# Lavender & Gin

*A Sapphic Historical Romance*

Abigail Aaronson

*For the queer community I love - especially my uncles C & M, and my grandfathers G & B. You showed me we've always been here, and I miss you every day.*

# Author Notes

This book is a queer historical romance set in the dangerous mafia underground of 1930 Detroit. It contains adult themes that may be disturbing to some readers, including:

Violence

Mob activity

Depictions of sex

For a detailed list of content notes, please see https://www.abigailaaronson.com/lgcontent

For up new releases, exclusive bonus content, advanced review opportunities, character art, access to my semi-secret blog, and more, subscribe to my newsletter: https://tinyurl.com/abigailaaronsonreadersclub

If you subscribe from this link, you'll get special Lavender & Gin bonus content: queer music that helped inspire the book, and book recommendations about queer speakeasies, The Purple Gang, and more.

If you enjoy this book, I would love for you to leave a review on your platform of choice. It's a huge help for me as an author, and you'll help fellow readers discover it!

You can find me on Instagram, Threads, and TikTok @abigailaaronsonwrites and on Facebook @abigailaaronsonauthor.

If you're a fan of queer historical romance, check out the Queer Historical Romance Instagram (@queerhistoricalromance) and Facebook Group.

# Chapter One

Missing in action. Kasia knew that's what they called it when a destroyed body was unidentifiable. But she'd always pictured her brother Andrew in suspended animation somewhere; still, naked, floating in deep water like a baby in the womb. It was easier that way. Staring into his closet, clothes covered in a light layer of dust, she was face-to-face with the truth. She ran gentle fingers over the remnants of him—the hanging suits, folded undershirts, his favorite hat, musty despite the care he'd taken to leave his things in perfect order.

He'd always been careful and detailed, and not only with his things. It showed in his drawings and paintings that covered their shared walls, a riot of landscapes with intricate blooms, loving portraits, sketches of household objects worn by constant use. But once he received his draft notice, he'd fallen farther into familiar habits; organization as a hedge against the coming chaos.

Kasia remembered him the day before he left. She sat on her bed, watching him take his clothes out of the drawer and re-fold them, just as he'd done every day since the letter came. The air between them was thick; Kasia could hardly breathe with the weight of it. She watched him in silence. She thought they'd already said all there was to say. Her mind kept turning to prayers for the damned.

Andrew paused his folding to look at her. His blond hair was carefully combed back; his strong, bold nose and deep-set eyes looked just like Kasia's. They both had their father's figure, tall and wiry. He was her physical mirror. In everything else, he was her opposite. Gentle, patient, quiet; he held the parts of her she was missing. Her heart twisted, knowing half of it was leaving with him.

"Can I ask you for something?" he said. His worried look made something inside Kasia desperate, clawing at the walls of her stomach. He could ask her for anything.

"Of course," she said. Her voice was hoarse. She cleared her throat, trying to hide it.

"Take care of our mother when I'm gone."

Their mother, Gosia, hadn't been well for years. Not since Kasia's father died when the twins were eight. She'd pulled into herself, wandering the house with dull eyes and slumped shoulders. Then her hands began to swell and ache. The pain made her volatile. She'd scream at Kasia and Andrew for slight sounds, imagined messes. As they grew, her temper evened; but in its place was a coldness and sharpness that pierced Kasia every time she and her mother shared a room. His request made every muscle tighten around her bones, bracing against it. "She doesn't want my help."

Andrew stood and sat next to her on her bed. He leaned his head against the wall. His eyes, usually the blue clarity of calm seas, were dark and anxious. Deep circles cut the space above his cheekbones. He hadn't been sleeping. Kasia hadn't either. "She needs it," he said. "She'll be worse when I'm gone."

They'd never said it aloud. But they both knew he got the best part of Gosia's mothering, while Kasia got scraps. Their mother was hard on both of them, but Andrew was Gosia's light in the dark. Maybe it made it easier for him to appreciate their mother's sacrifices, the way she ground her body into pieces to keep a roof over their heads and food in their mouths. For Kasia, it filled her with so much guilt there wasn't room for appreciation. She'd planned a hundred times to run away, taking the burden of herself with her. Andrew knew. He knew her every unspoken thought. But she knew him, too. She could read the weight in his words; he knew the unfairness of what he was asking.

"For as long as you can," he said when she was silent. He didn't ask her to promise. It almost made it worse. They took their promises to each other with the weight of an oath sworn to God. He knew a promise to look after their mother forever would be too much for Kasia to bear. But he was asking her to try.

Kasia felt the burning threat of tears. She held them back. "Alright," she said finally. "Until you're back."

Andrew didn't smile. Looking back, she thought he knew he wasn't coming home. He'd squeezed her hand, told her thank you, and moved back to his dresser to re-fold his clothes in silence.

At sixteen, Kasia had dropped out of school to work in the factory with their mother. The extra money helped. But after Andrew was drafted two years later, Gosia's health only worsened. Some shifts left Gosia bedridden. Kasia would leave porridge by her bed before she went to work her own shift, and when she came home, it was almost always untouched. The hollows under Gosia's eyes grew darker, her cheekbones sharper.

Then the letter came—the one that declared Andrew missing in action. Kasia watched Gosia read the government form and the letter from Andrew's commander that came with it. Her mother wailed, a sharp keening that split Kasia in half. One half wanted to collapse with her mother, wrap her arms around her despite the rareness of touch between them, let the unrelenting grief drown them both. The other half—the half that told Andrew she'd try—brought her mother to bed, where she'd laid for weeks.

For a year, her mother left her bed only for mass. One income wasn't enough for both of them. Not even with good factory wages. Not with the cost of her mother's doctor visits. Kasia fingered the sleeves of Andrew's hanging shirts. She'd thought long and hard about a way out for her and her mother. She'd spent four years at the factory now. The prospect of a lifetime there felt like staring down the barrel of a gun. How long until her body couldn't handle the labor, like Gosia?

She had a plan. She knew how to organize people. Kasia was good at that. She knew just how to make herself useful to the right people. The Purple Gang ran Detroit, and they made money from bootlegging hand over fist. They always needed help with deliveries, and they were willing to pay for a job well done.

But she knew she couldn't convince them as Kasia.

She slipped one of Andrew's shirts over her head. She'd bound her chest lightly with bandages; it didn't take much for her to flatten out the small curve there. Then his trousers and a suit jacket. She peered into a cloudy mirror over the dresser. The image startled her. She and Andrew had always looked alike; in his clothes, it was as though he'd

4

returned to say goodbye, on the other side of the glass. For a moment, she placed her fingers against the reflection.

The ache of missing him hit like a kick to her stomach, knocking the air out of her lungs. She looked away, took in deep gulping breaths as her knuckles went from red to white from the strength of her grip on the dresser. The room reeled beneath her. She wasn't sure how long it took to come back to herself. Seconds? Minutes? Time stretched relentlessly around her grief. It always did. She wanted to tear the clothes off, to shove the unbearable image of him in the mirror aside for good.

A strange, secret thing inside her spoke. She knew its voice. It had been with her as long as she could remember. It wasn't Andrew, but today it used his voice. Maybe she needed to hear him instead. *Look*, it demanded. It was a tone Andrew only used when he was annoyed with her. She raised her head.

Andrew's image met her in the mirror again. Except this time, it wasn't exactly Andrew. A warm flush rolled through her. Every stitch of the suit fell perfectly along her body. She straightened her shoulders, raised her chin. She'd never lacked in confidence—an unbecoming trait in a girl, immodest and confronting. But her confidence warred with discomfort. Dresses had always been unbearable. They felt as though they chafed her raw. The suit, though... she didn't have words to describe what she felt, but it had an undeniable correctness to it. The discomfort she'd carried for twenty years, something she'd thought of as an inevitable and endless compromise of womanhood, a lifetime companion to the burden of her illicit desires, burned away like morning mist. Not completely—fingers of fog still curled around the edges of her mind. But its disappearance washed her in a light she'd never known before.

The scissors she'd left on the dresser called to her. If she'd been intimidated by the thought of cutting her hair at first, the trepidation was gone now. Kasia hacked through the blonde locks until she had a close approximation of her brother's haircut. She'd need a barber to clean it up, but it would work for now. Kasia combed pomade through her hair, just like she'd seen Andrew do. Her head felt weightless. She traced her fingertips over the shortest places on the side. The prickle of cropped hair against her skin thrilled her.

She had never felt more like herself. It had never occurred to her that she *wasn't* herself before. Kasia had grown up hearing all the ways in which she didn't fit, where she fell short of expectations. And yet she'd never been able to be anything else. She'd long since decided not to try, even if she kept some pieces of herself hidden. But she wasn't herself, not completely. *This* was her. Her skin hummed with it. She was bursting out of herself like a ripe fruit splitting.

Kasia had only a minute to spend in her revelation before she remembered her purpose. This was only step one in her plan. There were so many to come. First, she had to tell her mother. The thought was sobering.

Kasia crept to her mother's bedroom. Gosia's eyes fluttered open when she heard the door. Her mother sprang upright, eyes wide. "Andrew? My Andrzejek?" Tears flooded her face. Kasia felt guilt heavy in her chest.

"Yes. From now on, yes," said Kasia.

Her mother cringed back at the realization that it was her daughter, not her missing son. Kasia had never felt more monstrous. She watched repulsion wash over her mother's face. Kasia fought the urge to shrink back, to make herself as small as she felt. She'd never put her plans into action if she turned back now. "Why?" Gosia said finally, her voice cracking.

"To take care of you," said Kasia. "To take care of us."

"I don't understand."

"You'll see." Kasia touched her mother's shoulder gently. It was stiff, resistant. "Kasia ran away to Chicago to marry. She's doing well, and happy, but too busy to visit."

Gosia stared at Kasia, her brows drawn hard together. She nodded, the motion slow and cautious.

Her cold acceptance of it made Kasia ache. She didn't expect support or gratitude for her choices. But some small part of her still wanted her mother's tenderness. She knew it was too much to hope for. Acknowledgement was the best she'd get. She steeled herself, shaped her voice into a firm wall between them. "Good," Kasia said. "I'm going out. Don't wait up for me." Her mother's expression was too hard to bear. She had to escape it.

Leaving the house brought relief. Freedom laid at her feet. Andrew could move in the world in ways Kasia couldn't. The familiar streets of Hamtramck were new again. The world was new again. A world she had plans for. A world that, for once, she could bend to her will. As long as she could keep her secret.

# Chapter Two

It hadn't taken long for Kasia to get used to her brother Andrew staring back at her in the mirror. A decade ago, she'd learned that there was no taking him on and off. They looked so alike; it felt as though she'd worn his face since birth. His clothes and his name came easy. Taking on Andrew's identity was, in fact, the only thing that *had* come easily to Kasia. Everything else she'd had to claw from the city's hands, spitting and thrashing.

It was why she liked to catch a few quiet moments in the warehouse before payday. Stuffing cash in envelopes was evidence of her success—hard-won, fickle, fleeting. Remembering how quickly it could turn tempered her satisfaction. She liked that. It kept her focused and sharp. It ensured she was just who she wanted to be as the gang trickled in.

Friday night always brought the boys into Hamtramck Gang headquarters—Czeslaw's family's paper supply business—rowdy and in high spirits. Henry tumbled into the room with Stan in a headlock. "Andrew!" Henry called as soon as he spotted Kasia at the desk. He released an unperturbed Stan, who flopped onto one of the room's well-worn couches. Henry headed straight to the record player, still talking over his shoulder to Kasia. "We get that new route?"

Stan answered for her with a groan. "Can't I get a drink before we talk business?"

"Get your drink, Stan," Kasia said. "I'm not discussing anything until everyone's accounted for."

Stan grinned and rifled through a big, industrial box of paper crammed next to the couch, looking for the gin and vodka hidden inside. He crowed triumphantly as he held a bottle aloft before opening it to take a swig.

Henry grabbed it from his hand. "Don't act like a fucking animal. Use a glass, you sap." Henry rummaged through another box for cocktail supplies. Once he'd poured a drink for Stan and himself, he raised in glass in Kasia's direction. "Na zdrowie."

Kasia always liked the boisterous mix of Polish and English when the gang met up. Not everyone's parents passed down the language of the fatherland, but most of the guys could understand it, and knew bits and pieces. The result was a unique patois that made Kasia immediately feel at home.

While the rest of the gang geared up to party, for Kasia, work came first. Kasia collected payments from deliveries daily, so no one "accidentally" mixed up their own money and hers—or rather, Sam's, her contact in the Purple Gang. The Purple Gang, the most powerful mob in Detroit, handled the bootlegging; they contracted the Hamtramck Gang for delivery. The ledger in front of her marked every man's name, his collections for the week, and what he was owed, each payment double-checked. Drinks in hand, Henry and Stan picked up their envelopes. Joe, Stevie, Ludwig, Pete, and Czeslaw grabbed theirs as they came in.

After everyone had their envelope of cash, Kasia waved a hand for the group to sit down. Henry silently placed a gin rickey next to her, and she allowed herself a single sip before continuing. "Stevie and Ludwig." She picked up a piece of paper Sam had passed off to her at their last meeting, written in code she'd come to know fluently. "I've got another paper route for you." It was their term for liquor delivery, used even in private. "Three new stops between Chicago Boulevard and Grand Street."

They mumbled an acknowledgement, more interested in the drinks in their hands. Joe, however, sat up straighter. "Chicago and Grand?"

Kasia, marking down a note in her ledger, didn't bother to look up at him. "That's what I said, Joe."

He stood, his chest puffed out. "That's my territory. You're telling me Stevie and Ludwig are getting a cut of my route?"

Kasia set down her pen and sat back, hands laced and settled against her stomach. She'd started sending Joe on deliveries alone when he couldn't stop causing problems with his partners—criticizing perfectly fine work, starting arguments, insinuating he was in charge. She'd hoped he'd learn a little humility when he realized how hard it was to work alone. Unfortunately, Joe seemed allergic to wisdom. "I didn't think I needed to say it outright, but since you're asking, that's exactly what I'm telling you."

Joe took a step towards her. A couple other guys shifted forward, ready to intervene. She raised two fingers, quietly signaling them to stay in place. "You can't give away my cut," Joe growled.

She gave him a hard stare. "You've 'lost' money you collected on that route twice now, and you think I'm inclined to give you more money to lose?"

"I didn't lose that money. I miscounted and I got it back to you. Besides, it was twice in three months."

"Yeah, 'miscounted.' And found mysteriously after you got back from the races. Besides, I'm just as disinclined to give you more responsibility if you've forgotten how to count." She waved him away. "Now sit back down before I give the rest of your route away and let you count your own fingers over and over until you remember how."

Joe's fingers twitched against his palms, the knuckles turning white. His eyes scanned the room, looking for backup. No one met his eyes. The Hamtramck Gang's connection with the Purple Gang was all Kasia's doing. The improbable alliance of a small group of Polish Catholic toughs and the biggest, most powerful gang in Detroit rested entirely on her shoulders and how thoroughly she'd won Sam over. And they all knew it. If something happened to Kasia, they'd be shit out of luck.

Joe leveled his glare around the room, muttering "Cowards" under his breath. Maybe she shouldn't have let it go, but he was backing down, taking his seat like she ordered. She went over a few more items of business, with less theatrics. By the time she wrapped up, the room's good mood was back. Pete hauled out the phonograph to show off the record he'd bought. Ludwig kept everyone's glasses full. Stan taught Henry the Texas Tommy, the two tripping over boxes and falling to the floor in peals of laughter.

"This is why you can't get a girl, Henry," Stevie called out. "You're a hulking bimbo with two left feet."

"Nah, he's just gotta stay off the dance floor. Show her your wallet instead," said Czeslaw.

Ludwig cackled. "Moths'll fly outta that thing if he tries, unless he stops spending all his coins on new togs."

"Hey, Andy," Henry said, peeling himself off the floor. "You got your eye on a girl these days?"

Kasia had learned not to freeze at the question. Whether or not the boys knew her secret—some were smarter than others—they liked to tease her about her seeming ambivalence towards women. "How do I have time for a broad when I'm busy babysitting you idiots?"

Joe gave a derisive snort from his chair in the corner, where he was still sulking. Kasia let it slide again, but he was raising her hackles. Overlooking disrespect would make her seem weak. She didn't like altercations with her boys, but he was pushing his luck.

Henry approached her table with a bottle of gin raised to refill her glass. She covered it with her hand. "No, thanks. You know I don't enjoy getting so bent I've got to ask the priest for forgiveness in the morning."

"You've got plenty of other things to ask forgiveness for, don't you?" Joe said. The chattering and laughter around them died down, everyone turning to watch the two of them.

Kasia slowly sat upright, shoulders tense. The room was silent now, the other men watching the two of them with wide eyes. She returned the barb with a warning smile. "I don't think there's anyone in this room with nothing to bring to confession, Joe. Including you."

"You know exactly what I'm talking about," Joe said. His eyes were glassy with liquor. "You're a fraud and a liar. An abomin—" Kasia closed the distance between them and smashed her glass into the side of his face. Joe screamed, glinting shards jutting from his cheek. They embedded into Kasia's hand as well, but adrenaline and rage kept her even. She pulled a switchblade from her pocket; with the press of her thumb, the knife shot from the handle, gleaming bright in the dull light.

"Hold him," she ordered. Pete and Stevie exchanged uncertain looks, but did as they were told. She used the knife to pry Joe's mouth open, the tip of it digging into the soft tissue behind his teeth. Kasia grabbed for his tongue. The muscle was slimy and panicked, hard to grasp between her fingers. She pulled it forward, the pink pointed end of it just outside his teeth. When she removed the knife, she sliced through the exposed tip before he could close his mouth and draw his tongue back.

Blood rushed from Joe's mouth and down his chin. His screams choked on the wet flow from his tongue. Kasia let him continue to thrash against Pete and Stevie's hold. The sounds of his pain echoed off the high walls. Everyone else was still, as if movement would make them her next target.

Joe's energy left him slowly. He stopped screaming, panting like a dog to recover the breath torn from him. When his eyes opened, Kasia held up the part of his tongue she'd removed. "Some things are better left unsaid, Joe." She threw the tissue to the ground. "Kept on the tip of your tongue. You can't do that," she wiped her knife on his pants before retracting the blade, "and I'll take the whole thing out."

She locked eyes with Ludwig. "Get him home and put him to bed." She waved a hand dismissively. "Everyone else, clean up and go home, too."

Still in silence, the rest of the crew worked—picking up glasses and rinsing them in the bathroom sink, hiding bottles back in boxes of paper, sweeping the glass off the floor. Kasia didn't bother to stay. She threw her jacket on and disappeared into the cold night.

# Chapter Three

At home, locked in the bathroom, Kasia picked shards of glass from her palm and rinsed the cuts. The night was still young, but she was exhausted. She thought of the brother whose identity she'd taken for her own. Her gentle, quiet brother, who would have been horrified at what she did in his name. Who had likely been horrified at what he'd been made to do in his own name at the end of his life. He'd never wanted to fire a bullet, as much as she'd never wanted to mend dresses. She slid to the floor, slumped against the door. "I'd be myself if they'd let me," she murmured. "You know. You would have been, too."

Thinking about Andrew made Kasia feel like she was shrinking into her childhood self. Small, strange, out of place. And lonely. Only Andrew made her feel at home in herself. Growing up, she'd constantly been on the wrong end of everyone else's judgment. Too outspoken, too rowdy, too boyish. Too rough around the edges. Too bad at school— for everything except math, which was useless for a girl except for balancing the household budget once she married. Family, neighbors, teachers, all had more criticisms than kind words for her. But not Andrew. He liked the way she stood up for him and other kids when they were targeted by bullies. He said she was smarter than anyone realized—he could tell by how she thought through things and strategized even their playground games. He was the only one to notice that she had a hard time reading because the words and letters all jumbled up for her, not because she wasn't trying. He thought she was strong and clever and tough. And for her part, she knew Andrew was the most thoughtful, kind, creative boy she'd ever seen. Not weak, not a sissy, like their father said before he died. Andrew's strength was subtle and quiet, like a boulder standing in a lake, impervious to the water's currents. He was simply himself, no matter what others said. He didn't fight people's opinions like she did. He was content in his own world, making drawings and paintings that still covered every inch of the walls in their room.

It was her room alone now. She couldn't stand the thought of being inside it at the moment. Not while she missed him with an ache that hollowed her out from head to toe.

She could hear the radio from the kitchen. Her mother was humming along with the tune, off-key. Kasia wiped her tear-streaked face before leaving the bathroom, following the tinny sound of the music.

Gosia sat at the table, sewing a torn coat pocket. She glanced up when Kasia entered. Her gaze lingered on Kasia's red eyes, but she looked back wordlessly at her mending, still humming. Despite the pain in her hands, Gosia tried to keep busy. Her stitches were slow, but practiced and even.

Kasia sat down with her, though she had nothing to say. She simply didn't want to be alone with her memories of

Andrew. What she wanted was to talk about him, to ask her mother what she remembered the most fondly. But she couldn't—not when, for her own mysterious purposes, her mother preferred they keep up the charade that she was Gosia's son. Even if she didn't, her mother didn't discuss feelings, or anything that might evoke them, if she could help it. Kasia stopped trying long ago.

The song on the radio ended, and Jerry Buckley's familiar announcer's voice replaced it. Gosia listened to the show, Buckley's commentary on local politics and social reform, almost as religiously as she went to mass. An interesting choice, Kasia thought, given that his focus on organized crime and corrupt city officials hit close to home. "Good evening from WMBC Detroit," the voice boomed in crisp trans-Atlantic tones. Kasia propped her chin in her good hand and gazed towards the speaker. "Perhaps you've seen today's Detroit Free Press article on the letter the good Reverend Hosaple, superintendent of the Michigan Anti-Saloon League, sent Representative Robert H. Clancy. Representative Clancy has characterized the fine folks holding the line of Prohibition as 'fanatical,' and has publicly mourned the deaths of the criminals injured by officers of the law in the course of their duties. The brave reverend reverses the claim. 'Don't you think the charges of fanaticism might well be laid against the congressman who seems to see red whenever some law-breaking wet is injured, but who can with utter complacency learn of the death or murder of faithful government officials?' the Reverend writes."

Gosia knotted the end of her stitches and held the needle aloft to cut the thread. The radio announcer continued. "If only degeneracy were limited to the congressman. Despite Mayor Bowles' campaign promise to clean up this city's streets—*your* streets—the Mayor has utterly failed to control the gangs that pollute your neighborhood with liquor and vice. Perhaps Detroit's new Police Chief Richard Harding will take up the mantle cast aside by our mayor. Today, Chief Harding announced increased manpower to interrupt supply chains for so-called speakeasies by targeting the illegal distributors of liquor that supply them. In a statement made on the steps of City Hall today, Mr. Harding said that he's not intimidated by the outlaws known as the Purple Gang that drive liquor smuggling in Detroit."

Kasia's mother glanced at her through her eyelashes. Much as her mother refused to discuss memories, emotions, or Kasia's real identity, she liked to pretend to be ignorant of her work. Still—she knew, and Kasia knew she knew. Kasia kept her gaze on the radio. Chief Harding's voice boomed out of it, strong and furious. "Violence and degeneracy have run rampant through our city. I will not allow a mob of miscreants to threaten the lives and livelihoods of the decent, God-fearing citizens of Detroit," he said. Kasia could picture him pointing emphatically at a crowd of jour-nalists and onlookers. "This country voted for Prohibition because we recognize that enslavement to liquor brings debauchery not just to our cities, but through your home's threshold. We cannot allow racketeers to undo the great strides we've made to protect our city from the harms caused by alcohol, nor can we look away when they main-tain their power through brutality."

Kasia tucked her bandaged hand between her legs, still avoiding her mother's gaze. She'd seen the new chief in the papers. Articles lauded him as "The Incorruptible Chief Harding." But with the power the Purple Gang held, cops were usually more of an inconvenience than a threat.

"Wasn't the police commissioner fired for conducting raids while the Mayor was out of town?" Kasia said, trying to sound casual. "Seems unwise for a new police chief to follow the same path."

Her mother set down her coat and returned her needle to a pincushion. "Mayor Bowles won the election by promising to reduce crime in the city," she said curtly. "Someone should hold him to his word. You'd know if you paid attention."

Kasia scowled. It had been a long night; she didn't need her mother's disapproval, much less to pretend that her mother's obsession with Buckley's show wasn't an attempt to distance herself from Kasia and her work. She kept a roof over their heads and food on their table, not to mention a few comforts they'd never been able to afford before she started the gang. Her mother never fussed when Kasia paid the bills. It made these moments, when her mother feigned moral superiority, especially grating. "Goodnight, then," she said, pushing her chair back from the table with a sharp scrape.

Gosia fixed her eyes on the wall behind her. Her sudden stillness made Kasia pause as well. Gosia worried her lower lip between her teeth. "Be careful," she said in return. "*Nie wywołuj wilka z lasu.*" *Don't call the wolf from the forest.*

It was the closest she'd ever come to acknowledging Kasia's work. An uncomfortable feeling quickly overtook Kasia's surprise: being on the receiving end of her mother's concern. Kasia hovered in the door, unsure how to respond. She rapped her knuckles twice against the doorframe, unconsciously biting her lip in a mirror of her mother. She had nothing to say; she went to bed.

# Chapter Four

Sam was waiting for Kasia at the deli. He always sat in the same booth, and the coffee in front of him was always steaming fresh. It didn't matter where they were meeting, or how punctual she was—Sam got there first. She'd showed up an hour early once, determined to wait for him for a change, and there he was. He'd scolded her for not being punctual, which she thought was a little unfair, even if it was *technically* true.

Kasia slid into the booth across from him and threw a paper bag of cash down between them. It wasn't subtle, but Sam didn't need to be subtle. The Purple Gang ran Detroit, and Sam, along with a handful of other guys he'd met in his school days in Paradise Valley, ran the Purple Gang. Legend had it their name came from two shopkeepers when the Purples were still young, making their money through extortion and petty crime. As the story went, one shopkeeper said to the other, "These boys are not like other children of their age. They're tainted, off-color."

"Yes," replied the other shopkeeper. "They're rotten, purple like the color of bad meat. They're a Purple Gang."

Kasia always liked the story, even if Sam never confirmed it. Maybe because she felt tainted and off-color herself, and just like the Purples, built a life out of it. Maybe that was why Sam had taken a shine to her, too. She reminded him of his younger self. That, and she was good at making him money. They were useful to each other. She'd turned the Hamtramck Gang into a solid organization. But they were small, and their collaboration with the Purple Gang offered far better opportunities and protection than they'd ever be able to afford on their own.

Sam stuck the cash in his inner coat pocket. He didn't bother to count it. Kasia had proven herself fastidious week after week. She'd been straightforward about any difficulties the gang ran into, solved problems quickly, and every dollar Sam expected always made it into his hands. In another life, she might have been a manager's favorite in an office, climbing the ladder of the American dream. Instead, she was transporting bootlegged liquor to underground bars and clubs. At least it paid well. Sam sat back and took a deep sip from the mug in front of him. "Any issues with delivery?"

She shook her head. "No. Nothing now that the new clients know not to try anything on us they wouldn't on your boys." The Purple Gang had a reputation for ruthlessness. Part of her job was making sure it stayed that way, even if the Hamtramck Gang were unofficial representatives. Sam nodded in return. There was silence between them. Kasia pulled a pack of cigarettes from her pocket. Their business was done, but it was an excuse to chat with Sam. He'd grown to like her company.

Sam winced as she placed a cigarette in her mouth. "Jesus, kid. You know how I feel about those soft packs. If you won't use a case, at least turn the cigarettes around."

"Why would I do that?" Kasia knew the answer.

They'd had this conversation a dozen times. But Sam liked something to mentor her on. A little stubbornness was enjoyable for him, as long as it didn't impact cash flow.

"Every step you take packs the cigarettes. Settles the tobacco down a little further. I don't know why these fucking companies pack them the wrong way."

"Why not just turn the pack upside-down in my pocket, if it's such a big deal?"

"You want loose tobacco all over your jacket?" Sam pushed his cigarette case to the middle of the table and opened it, showing off. He took a cigarette out and held it aloft. "Attention to detail. Even in the little things." He placed the end in his mouth and flicked open a lighter, held the flame until the cigarette burned red. Sam pointed at Kasia with the cigarette between his fingers. "That's what you need if you want to become a Purple."

Kasia's shoulders tensed. She contracted her gang with the Purples; partners in crime, but separate entities. For ten years, she'd wanted in. *Being* a Purple, a real Purple, not hired muscle, had been her dream since the beginning. She wanted the name, but more than that, she wanted the opportunity to rise in the ranks. She wanted the higher pay. The additional protection for her boys and her neighbors. When she was younger, it was her only measure of success. But Sam didn't let anyone outside his neighborhood in. Not easily, at least. And no matter how useful she proved herself to be, he always seemed to think she was more useful exactly where she was. She tried not to care. He dangled the possibility in front of her, anyway. And despite knowing better, wanting it held her in a vise grip. Sam knew. It was why he did it.

"I think I've demonstrated my attention to detail

enough for you, Sam," Kasia said. It was hard to keep the defensive edge from her voice.

The man chuckled. He clapped a hand over her shoulder. "You're a good kid. You do good work." He took a drag from his cigarette. "I'm just saying you deserve the same attention to the rest of your life."

Kasia flicked the end of her cigarette into the ashtray between them. "There's no 'rest of my life,' Sam. You own it." She tugged her cheek into a half-smile, and Sam roared with laughter.

"That's on you. Get out to a gin joint. Meet some dolls. Try to loosen up a little. You're still young. Act like it."

"I'm thirty."

"Thirty's a kid. Thirty's nothing."

"I'm not looking to settle down."

"Who said anything about settling down?" Sam shook his head. "Take my advice and put off marriage as long as you can. It's easier that way."

Kasia leaned back in her seat, threw an arm across the back of the booth. "Women are too much trouble?"

"No." Sam's face settled into seriousness as he leaned across the table. "Because if you have a family, it gives you more to lose." He looked around, dropped his voice. Sam was never afraid of being overheard, but he almost whispered now. "You don't know. You've got your mother to take care of, sure. But you don't know the kind of fear that comes when you've got a wife, a kid or two. That kind of fear, it gets in the way. It makes you fucking stupid sometimes. But you can't get rid of it. It haunts you." He sat back up, his voice returning to normal. "So, have your fun. Just don't get attached."

Kasia was silent, thrown by what had just passed between them. It was a side of Sam she'd never seen, and she didn't know what to do with it. She bit back a laugh. What was she supposed to say? *I'm an invert. A family of my own is a fantasy.* She couldn't imagine a woman willingly attaching herself to her, between her job and her secret. One or the other, sure. The gang had better luck with women than they had any right to, if anything. But both, on top of being a homosexual? She blew a long, slow stream of smoke from her nose before finally settling on, "Don't worry about me."

Sam chuckled. "I never do. That's what I like about you."

Kasia stubbed out her cigarette. Sam's moods were fickle. She felt as though she'd passed a test, even if she didn't know what it was, and wanted to end their meeting on a good note. "See you next week, Sam."

Sam grunted a response. She left, pausing outside the deli's doors to brace against the biting wind while she buttoned her coat. Her neck suddenly prickled, a hot flush against the cold. It stopped Kasia in her tracks. She pulled another cigarette from her pocket, using the motion to disguise her glance at the surrounding city block.

Across the street, a man rested his shoulder against the bricks behind him. He stared down into a newspaper. As Kasia watched, he glanced back up, then quickly back down again. He thumbed through the pages before lifting the paper to cover his face.

The buzz in her neck spread through Kasia's body, pulling every muscle into tight readiness. Her body, with a knowledge deeper than consciousness, knew she was being watched. Kasia tugged her hat over her eyes. She could confront him, but what good would that do? Confrontation —especially on the street in broad daylight—invited unwanted attention, and possibly the police. And if Sam was his actual target, she didn't want to make herself more memorable.

Instead, she walked down the street in the opposite direction from home. She'd deliver a message to Sam with her suspicions later. In the meantime, she had to lose anyone who might be following her.

# Chapter Five

Kasia was tallying her ledger in the back of the warehouse when she heard a knock at the door. Her head shot up. The boys rarely bothered to knock when she was working, familiarity breeding impoliteness. She placed a hand over the pistol on her hip before calling, "Come in."

The door opened hesitantly. Pete peeked through. "Andy?"

"Jesus Christ, Pete." Kasia leaned back in her chair, hand easing off the gun at her side. "I thought we had cops in the joint. What do you need?"

Pete took a few hesitant steps forward. "It's Christopher." Her cousin's name shot annoyance through her. "He got in a scrap with another kid." That explained Pete's hesitation and sudden concern with propriety. He was delivering bad news.

"How bad was it?" Christopher was a problem, bored and restless with a habit of picking fights. He was also in the habit of getting Kasia to bail him out of trouble.

"It got broken up pretty quick. But they were drunk, and the cops hauled them both in."

Kasia sighed. She could picture Christopher telling him to tell her, confident she could make it all go away. And she probably could. She didn't want to; she only had so many strings to pull. But if she didn't, she'd be hearing about it from her aunt, and double from her mother. She stood and pulled on her coat. "Where's he being held?"

\* \* \*

February nights had a way of seeping into Kasia, festering and inevitable. The cold was only half of it. Something about the filthy, slate-colored days fading early into darkness burrowed deeper than the cold could reach. Favors were as inevitable as the grim chokehold of the weather, of course. But it didn't stop the burn of resentment she felt.

The police station was frantic and bright compared to the Detroit evening she'd left outside. Kasia stripped off her overcoat and smoothed the wide lapels of the grey wool suit beneath. Her newsboy hat—her brother's favorite—was wind-battered and askew. She carefully tugged it back into place. Even with cops on her payroll, it paid dividends to look proper. Kasia squinted into the light until her eyes settled on a familiar face. Officer Ward stood behind the wide wooden desk at the back of the room, shuffling papers. She caught his attention with a cough and jerked her head towards a quiet corner.

He nodded back. Kasia watched him scan the room as he approached, his shoulders high and rigid. "Andrew," Officer Ward murmured as he reached her. "What are you doing here?"

Kasia gave his hand an authoritative shake. "Good to see

you too, John." The policeman winced. It sent a ripple of satisfaction through her. "I'm here for a favor."

The man cleared his throat and glanced behind him, towards a small cluster of his colleagues. They were too busy to notice the conversation, an officer on the phone frantically but inaudibly directing the rest. "I think I'm doing you boys plenty of favors."

*Łaska Pana na pstrym koniu jeździ.* Her mother's phrase came to mind every time she pushed her luck. *The Lord's grace rides on a dappled horse.* Favors from the powerful were a fickle thing. "And we're always grateful for your help." She reached into her jacket and placed a wad of cash in his chest pocket. Kasia smiled, trying to put the officer at ease. Instead, he shifted uncomfortably. Their relationship had always been based on the stick and the carrot, the carrot being money to look the other way as her gang funneled booze into underground bars and clubs. But maybe she'd gone too hard on the stick when they first met. Blowing up his car may have been a little dramatic. "Besides, it's a small one. Over and done in a minute."

She leaned in closer. Officer Ward shuffled a step back. He was a short man, she towered over him. "My cousin Christopher.... You've got him back there in the drunk tank. Might be under his given name, Krzysztof." She raised a brow. "Or you know, something along those lines. Detroit's finest can't spell in Polish." Officer Ward didn't laugh at her joke. Fair enough. She wasn't paying him to stroke her ego. "Anyway, he got into a fight with some other kid. They're both eighteen—you know how it goes. His ma's in bad health, and I want to get him back in bed before she's up."

Officer Ward released a long breath. "What about the other kid?"

"Fuck the other kid. Do what you want with him. Keep him in, send him home. It's no skin off my nose."

"You gonna take care of him yourself once he's out?" The officer paled.

"Is that what you think of me?" She clapped a hand on his shoulder. "Listen, he's not my business. You know my business. You think I make money roughing up a teenager for the crime of being a moron? His father will do it himself for free."

"Ward," a cop yelled from over the desk. "We got a paddy wagon coming in."

Officer Ward swore under his breath. "Look, I'll get your cousin out tonight," he whispered. "No paperwork, no problems. But I've got to deal with this first. Wait out here."

Kasia pushed the brim of her hat up with her thumb. "Sure, sure. But don't take too long. You know I'm not a patient man."

The officer disappeared into a back room. Kasia settled onto a bench in the waiting area, one arm slung over the backrest. She worked off the collar attached to her shirt and threw it into her lap before unbuttoning the first couple of buttons around her neck, stretching her head from side to side. Kasia was used to late nights, but she preferred not to spend them sitting in a police station. She crossed her ankle over her knee, her foot on the floor tapping out her irritation.

Suddenly, the room filled with bodies and noise. Cops hauled in groups of garish revelers in a colorful, indignant stream. Plenty were rich kids in their twenties from the nice parts of the city, coming to slum it from their safe, staid enclaves in Rosedale Park and English Village. She could tell because several were threatening the officers escorting them to the holding tanks with their daddy's wrath. A couple of others cried their lives were over. Kasia doubted that. Their parents were drinking in private clubs while their kids drank in speakeasies. They'd be pissed their kids got caught, but not with what they were doing. They had money, and with money came the power to make it all go away. Just like what she was doing for Christopher—not that they'd appreciate the comparison.

Then the crowd being hauled in shifted. There were people of all ages, with clothes indicating they came from rich families and poor, and everything in between. Some were men in beaded dresses, women in suits. Kasia thought they might've broken up a black and tan speakeasy. Instead, they'd raided a pansy bar.

She buttoned her shirt back up and replaced the collar. No one was paying attention to her, but the proximity of the cross-dressers made her nervous—as if standing too close meant they'd call out her secret, say *you're one of us* and blow the whole tenuously held together charade into pieces. Sure, the families in her neighborhood might have thought it was awfully convenient that Gosia's daughter eloped to Chicago right before Kasia's twin brother returned from the war after being declared missing for so long. But "Andrew" came back generous. He employed their sons and made sure everyone's grandma was comfortable in the winter. He protected the neighborhood and homes from vandals and theft. Kasia gave them decent reasons to forgive the coincidence. The rest of the world, though—they had their own reasons to tear her down.

Kasia crossed her arms and slid down in her seat, tugging her hat back over her eyes. The flow of arrested patrons parted. A woman appeared in their wake, shoulders back and movements slow and deliberate even while her hands were handcuffed behind her. The officer escorting her was young, and blushing brightly right up to the tips of his ears. Her dress was an even brighter red than his face, in a silk that slid around each curve of her hips and waist as she moved. Bold, swooping curls of embroidered shining beads swept the fabric and hung in fringe from the hem. Unlike the others in custody, she'd somehow taken the time to retrieve a fur stole that was wrapped loosely around her shoulders. Her face wore impeccable make-up and an unabashed, mischievous smirk.

Kasia couldn't take her eyes off her. The woman noticed, tossed her dark, curled bob out of her face, and drew her own gaze down Kasia's body, now upright and at attention in her seat. The woman in red winked, and Kasia felt herself flush almost as much as the escorting officer. She looked at her feet, shielding her blush behind her hat.

The woman and officer stopped at the desk, in front of another cop observing the proceedings. The young policeman cleared his throat. "Sir? This woman requests that we call Chief Harding."

The officer behind the desk gave the woman a hard look, and she tilted her head in reply. "Sophia Worley. I'd shake your hand, but I'm afraid I'm not able to extend you the courtesy. I'm a personal friend of Chief Harding and his wife, Margaret. I have no doubt that he'll be able to untangle this misunderstanding." The two policemen exchanged a doubtful look, and Sophia's smile widened. "I stayed with them at their summer house on Grand Lake last year. We became intimate friends. I'm sure he'd like to know I'm here."

The officer behind the desk heaved a sigh. "Fine. Put her in the meeting room and stay with her. I'll call the Chief." He pointed at Sophia. "But if you're lying to an officer, ma'am, that's an offense that I'll make sure we add to your charges."

She tossed her hair again, her easy smile returning. "Of course, I wouldn't expect anything less."

The young officer brought her to a room just next to the desk and gestured her inside, as if she were waiting for an appointment. Officer Ward passed by and glanced in; he spoke in low tones to the officer now on guard outside the door. Kasia rose from the bench and gestured him over. Officer Ward approached warily. "I'll have your cousin out in just a minute. We're booked full. No one will even miss him."

"Yeah. Good. Look—who's the dame in the red who just came in? She says she knows the Chief."

"Sophia Worley."

"Sure, I heard that much. But what's her deal? How does she know the Chief?"

Officer Ward glanced around and leaned in. "I don't know how she knows the Chief, and if I speculate, it's my job on the line. Because we just busted her at a bar for inverts."

Kasia glanced at the milling crowd. "Yeah, I gathered that." Her eyes narrowed. "All of them? Those kids from out of town?"

The policeman shook his head, looking grim. "You're not gonna believe it. People come from all over to the pansy bars. It's the new craze. First, they came for all the Black clubs. Now it's all places full of cross-dressers and homos. What are we coming to, you know?"

Kasia's steady gaze seemed to tell him he wasn't finding a sympathetic audience, and he stopped talking. "People want new experiences and familiar drinks. They always have," she said. "Young people are always going to find ways to piss off the old folks. We did it, they'll do it, their grandkids will do it. As long as they're doing it in a place I'm supplying, I don't care."

Officer Ward puffed with unexpressed moral superiority. "That's what you think, but you gotta be careful out there. You never know what you're getting with these girls. Every man thinks he can sniff out a bad character, you know? But I've seen it all, and some of these inverts, you can't even tell. There's pretty girls out here trawling the bars for other women, just like men."

Kasia reached into her coat and slipped another bill into his pocket, nestled tight against the others she'd given him earlier. She hoped it would soothe his discomfort and encourage him to wrap up the conversation. "Why do you think I steer clear of 'em all? Nothing but trouble."

Officer Ward nodded. Nothing like complaining about women to establish a sense of camaraderie between men. "I'll go get your cousin."

Kasia sat back down and watched the room clear. After all the noise and bustle, it was almost eerily calm. It didn't stay that way. Soon Kasia witnessed the Chief himself burst into the room, the ties of the robe thrown over his pajamas trailing behind him. He spoke in low, angry tones to the officer behind the desk before flying into the meeting room where Sophia was waiting. At the door, he shooed the guarding officer away before shutting it firmly behind him.

Kasia couldn't help but wonder what was going on inside. Chief Harding ran out of his house in his pajamas for this woman. That was a pretty special attachment for a married man. Knowing what Sophia had on Chief Harding would be very useful information. The kind of information Sam would be interested in knowing, too. And possibly, finally, earn her the right to be a Purple.

Someone from down the hall called out a name, and the

officer behind the desk left his post to answer. She knew it would be her only opportunity. Kasia walked to the door, glancing carefully down the empty hallways, and peeked into the room through the door's small, square window.

Sophia was calm and poised in her seat at the head of the table. The Chief had unlocked her handcuffs, and she was tracing one nail, empty half-moons adjoining red at the base, against the table's scratched surface. Based on his entrance, Kasia had expected to see Chief Harding furious; instead, he was standing in a slump, his head in his hands. He sank slowly into a chair, and Sophia patted his arm. She stood and adjusted the fur that had fallen off her delicate shoulder. Kasia ducked, afraid she'd look towards the door, and scrambled back to the waiting area. Moments later, Sophia appeared. She walked—hips swaying, shoulders back, like Kasia imagined Cleopatra walking—towards the door. Kasia waited for another glance her way, holding her breath. But Sophia didn't spare her a single flutter of her carefully beaded eyelashes.

# Chapter Six

When Kasia rode along for deliveries, it was always with Stan and Henry. It helped keep them on track. They were both cut-ups, feeding on each other's jokes, easily distracted. That would've been fine if it were just paper in the back of their painted trucks. Since bottles of booze were tucked in along with the ledgers, typewriter paper, stationary and reams of newsprint, Kasia preferred attention to the environment.

"I saw Christopher this morning," Stan told her as she lifted herself into the seat between the two men. "Little man has quite a shiner. Didn't look too humbled, though."

"He won't learn anything," Kasia said, resisting the urge to spit. Her lack of sleep left her with a splitting headache, thanks to her cousin. That's what she preferred to blame for her insomnia, at least. She'd spent half the night tossing and turning, unable to get the woman in red out of her head. "I should've let him cool his heels in a cell for a bit. Maybe then he'd learn some self-restraint."

"It just takes time," Henry said as he swung the truck

door shut next to him. "Life'll teach him. It teaches every-one. You were different at his age, too."

A second of awkward silence passed between them. Unlike Joe, Kasia trusted Henry's intention behind the words. Whether or not he knew she was Kasia—and she suspected he did, he wasn't a fool—he'd have meant it sincerely. But it was treading close to the truth. "I was never that bad," she said, hedging. She could hear the echoes of Officer Ward's rant in her voice, an irritating familiarity. "Alright, maybe I was. But I had to establish myself in the neighborhood."

"No one thought you had it in you," Stan said. Kasia was less sure that Stan understood she was not, in fact, her brother. He was a reliable worker, but he spent most of his time with his head in the clouds. "You proved them all wrong." She appreciated the pride in his voice. Stan and Henry were beside her in the early days, when they made most of their money with a little breaking and entering outside the neighborhood while protecting their own neigh-borhood from the same.

Henry had the grace to change the subject. He started in about how he thought wider trousers were coming into style in the new decade. His fashion opinions always got Stan heated, probably because Stan's only opinions on clothes were that they should be cheap and durable.

Their bickering blended into the roar of the engine as Kasia watched the road ahead. Sophia Worley, in her red dress, sprang into her mind like Aphrodite bursting from the ocean. Kasia lingered on it; the drape of the fabric around her body, the spray of dark curls around her cheeks, the wink she'd tossed her from dark-rimmed green eyes. Something about the woman drew her.

She wanted to know what it was Sophia had on Chief Richard Harding.

Extracting that information might hold the overenthusiastic officer at bay. If Sophia could use it, so could she. Whatever it was, it had already proved its efficiency. If Sophia was hanging around pansy bars, maybe Kasia could use it to get her to cooperate. It was information plenty of people wouldn't want to come out.

The thought turned Kasia's stomach a little. It was too close to her own truth for it to feel comfortable. Kasia avoided places where inverts met. That same feeling she'd had in the police station, that they'd see right through her disguise as Andrew, kept her away.

She'd thought about it before. Ever since she learned these places existed when she started delivering for the Purples. The difference she'd felt since childhood, that she'd hidden as Kasia and felt compelled to hide even as Andrew, had a name. There were women like her, who met other women like her, who danced and kissed and fucked like she'd dreamed of doing. She never wondered if her disguise as her brother brought it out. Kasia had known since girlhood that her heart didn't beat faster for boys. It did for Rose Milinski, though, a classmate with soft black curls and an ethereal countenance. She was a favorite among the neighborhood boys, who expressed their interest by flicking her skirt and catcalling her on her way home from school. Kasia started walking her home. If anyone so much as gave Rose an untoward look, Kasia punched their nose in.

Then the war began, and Kasia left school to work in the factory with her mother. The last she'd heard, Rose caught the attention of some steel baron's son and was whisked off to New York when the family business expanded. Kasia wondered if Rose ever thought of her. It was the closest thing Kasia had felt to love.

Now that she was Andrew, she avoided the company of women. It was a risky move, prone to outing her in another way entirely by making Andrew seem a bit queer himself. She threw herself into her work, excused her disinterest as ambition. The risk paid off, as risks usually did when she took them. Aside from some gentle ribbing about her celibacy from the guys, it seemed to put off any inconvenient questions.

Henry nudged her with his elbow. They'd parked at the end of a shop-lined street. Their stop was a small, secret bar above a milliner. Officially, they delivered tissue paper for packaging.

"Let's get a move on," Kasia said, as though she hadn't been lost in thought moments earlier. Henry and Stan were good-natured enough to let it pass without comment. They jogged to the back of the truck and started unloading boxes.

Kasia stayed in the car, hands clasped over her stomach. Her brain turned over the possibilities of Sophia Worley.

She had to find her first. And then she had to make her willing to share. If there was one thing Kasia liked, though, it was a challenge.

# Chapter Seven

Over the decade she'd spent as Andrew, her brother's clothes were prone to moth holes and ripped seams. They were also well out of fashion. She bought new clothes now and then, just to keep from looking too sloppy. But Kasia was still most comfortable in Andrew's things. It had a way of keeping him close.

Despite her own preferences, she always paid attention to others' choices. Something about Sophia Worley told Kasia she had money. Maybe it was the elaborate beading on the dress, or the longer hemline that was coming back into fashion. She could clearly afford to stay in style.

If she had money, she probably had friends with money. People with money stuck together. Better yet, people with money had a way of making themselves known. They dressed to show off. They assumed people knew their name. They considered themselves important. Who they knew was part of the atmosphere they cultivated around themselves. If Kasia could figure out who Sophia knew, she could find her.

It was time to take Sam's advice. She couldn't get into

wealthy private clubs—even as a liquor distributor. Those weren't her routes. But like Officer Ward had lamented, plenty of rich people liked to go slumming. Excitement and safety weren't always compatible. They liked to play at being on the fringes, with the artists, the musicians, and the radicals. They roamed Black and immigrant neighborhoods looking for risqué pleasures and then returned home to beds turned down by their housemaids. Sophia's pleasure was apparently the pansy clubs.

There were two Kasia had heard of through her work. One was on 3$^{rd}$ Street in Midtown. Another was on Park and West Columbia. She knew there were others, but not by name. Neither were far from Paradise Valley and Black Bottom: Black neighborhoods full of thriving businesses, including more bars and nightclubs than she could count, pansy bars among them. Paradise Valley and Black Bottom were popular destinations for revelers, and the diverse residents of the city descended on them for their fix of good jazz and flowing liquor. Like Harlem in New York, the neighborhood was home to countless Black creatives and intellectuals, giving it a bohemian atmosphere despite the intense poverty and overcrowding forced on the residents by redlining and exploitative pay for Black workers. And like Harlem, it housed pansy clubs that primarily served the neighborhood's underground queer community before slummers decided their bars were the next hot thing. But it wasn't her delivery territory, and she didn't know anyone familiar with the Black pansy clubs to ask.

That meant Kasia had few options to choose from. She went with the club on Park—farther away from home, where she was less likely to be spotted.

She stood on the corner, smoking, as she watched people file into the restaurant that fronted the club. From a distance, she couldn't tell much about the patrons. Dressed to the nines, certainly. Kasia sauntered across the street and posted up next to the restaurant door. Couples entered and left. A group passed her, and Kasia paused, searching faces and listening for tells that they weren't here for the daily special. She watched them take seats through the window.

The next cluster of revelers came. Two men in the group caught her eye. One held his hand on the other's back. Subtle, companionable, unremarkable, but tender. The touch seemed to speak of something deeper. It made Kasia's chest ache to watch. She pushed the feeling aside and tailed them into the restaurant, close enough to be mistaken for part of their group.

She couldn't hear what they said to the staff, but soon she was trailing behind, through a set of doors next to the kitchen marked as a supply closet. The back of the closet had been torn down, leading to a spacious but crowded back room. A bar ran partway down the wall. Kasia slipped between jostling arms, around the dancefloor, and took a seat on a high stool.

She tried to hide how shaken she was to be there. As she'd passed the dancers, she'd noticed another woman in a suit, tight over unbound breasts, dancing with a woman who rested her head on her shoulder. Their eyes were closed, lost in the sway of their pressed hips, hands clasped and arms wrapped tight. It drove the confidence she'd gained from her successful, surreptitious entry right out of her. She could almost feel the press of a soft body against her own, an illusory scent of soap and perfume and hot skin teasing her nostrils. Watching the dancing women carved up her insides, replaced what was there with a sick, envious ache. But she tore her eyes away reluctantly.

"A gin rickey, please," she told the bartender. She didn't

like how raspy and anxious her voice sounded. Unfazed, the man behind the bar poured her the drink, and she slid cash across the bar's slick wood in return.

Encouraged by the glass in her hand, Kasia turned back to the crowd. A cluster of men laughed together, and Kasia could pick out a couple of high, free voices among them. The tallest woman she'd ever seen, dressed primly and with a cloche hat pulled over her hair, interrupted and embraced each man in turn. One spun her around, hand raised high over his head to accommodate the length of hers, and whistled.

The permeating camaraderie reminded her of the paper supply's back room. But while her gang's headquarters held the same sense of familiarity and excitement on a Friday night, the pansy bar lacked the edge of threat. Instead, it seemed to burst with warmth, hum with the high of liberty.

The feeling was disquieting. It made Kasia shift in her seat, uncomfortable.

She turned back to the bartender. "Excuse me." The man glanced at her, barely, and held up a finger. After he finished pouring a drink, he came to her call.

"Something else?" He pointed to her still-full glass.

"I'm looking for someone," Kasia said.

The bartender raised an eyebrow. "What sort of someone are you looking for?" His eyes scraped down her figure, questioning. "We take all kinds here."

Suddenly, Kasia's suit felt suffocating. She steeled herself and cleared her throat. "A particular someone. Sophia Worley."

"Sophia?" Surprise passed over the bartender's face before he could pull it back. His eyes narrowed. "How do you know Sophia?"

"I don't," Kasia admitted. The man was already suspicious. Lying would entrench him further in doubt. "I saw her at a police station after a raid."

"You're a cop?"

Kasia smiled. This concern she could understand. She pulled cash from her pocket, drained her drink, and placed the money under the edge of her empty glass. She slid it across the counter towards him. "No. I'm not a cop. I just know a cop that's useful. I think Sophia knows a useful cop, too."

The bartender took the cash and placed it behind the counter. Still, his expression didn't change. "Sophia knows a lot of people."

Kasia pulled out a few more dollars. "I'll take another one when you get a chance." She laid the money out in front of her, far more than a drink was worth. The man filled her glass again and took the cash, with a hopefully more agreeable sense of suspicion. "She's a very beautiful woman," Kasia said after holding up the glass in thanks. "She piqued my interest." It was the truth, and the truth had a way of disarming.

The bartender drummed his fingers against the wood. She could feel him about to relent. It was always a favorite moment, the delicious second before she changed someone's mind, brought them into her plans. "Talk to James." He pointed towards the group of men Kasia watched earlier. She thought he was pointing towards a man on the end, tall and tan, balding at the temples but full of healthful glow. "They're close. Tell him what you want. He might pass along a message for you."

Kasia thanked him and handed over a final dollar. It paid to keep people happy, or at least content with their exchange. She slid off her stool and approached the man the bartender had pointed out.

"James?" she said.

The man turned to look at her, face scrunched in confusion. "Yes?"

Kasia held out a hand. "Andrew Kasowski." James's hand pressed into hers, and she shook it firmly. "I hear you're a friend of Sophia Worley."

"I am," James said cautiously. He looked Kasia up and down. "How do you know her?"

"I have a business proposal for her," Kasia said.

"You're in luck. I'm her business partner," James replied. "Is this about the club?"

"This club?"

"No, our club. The Lavender. We open next week."

If it was another pansy club, Kasia realized Sophia might be less precious about the reason for her arrest than she'd anticipated. But it was a stroke of good fortune that James's relationship with Sophia involved a club at all. "As a matter of fact, I run a beverage supplier." James looked askance at Kasia. Alright, so he knew well enough that the Purples were the only suppliers around. "The delivery, I mean. Do you work with Sam?"

"We've got a contact for beverages that goes by Junior," James said.

Junior. Probably Jacob Junior, one of Sam's colleagues. She'd have to convince Sam to take the account instead. Junior wouldn't be happy. "Junior, sure. We deliver for him, too." It wasn't an entire lie. Her crew helped out when Junior's contracted team fell short. Making it a regular gig, though, was another matter.

"You're here to tell us you're on our delivery team?" James said.

This was getting messier than Kasia intended. She could feel herself digging a hole she'd rather not have to crawl her way back out of. "Not exactly. I hope to deliver to your club, and if I do, I promise you'll be in excellent hands. But the business I have with Sophia is personal. I don't know her, but I'd like to."

A light of recognition flickered in James's eyes. "I'll tell you what," he said. "Come by the Lavender once we've opened. I'll make an introduction."

It was good enough. Kasia offered her hand again. "Thanks, James. Good luck with the opening."

# Chapter Eight

Sam wasn't happy with her request. "You're asking me to poach money from Junior?" The man tapped an unlit cigarette aggressively against the table. "Jesus, Andrew, why the hell would I pick that fight? Don't you know by now I've got enough on my plate? Junior's been on edge ever since the Chicago massacre. Convinced Capone's sabotaging everything he's got. And you want me to take his route? Your role is to make my business easier. Don't forget it."

Kasia expected him to dig his heels in. Now she had to tip her hand, just a little, to get him hooked. "That's what I'm hoping to do, Sam." She stilled her jittering foot. She couldn't afford to convey anything but assurance. "One of the proprietors knows the Chief of Police."

"Harding?" That caught Sam's attention. But only for a moment. "So, she knows Harding. I don't see how that helps me."

"I think she's got something on him," Kasia said. "Something that keeps him in her pocket."

"Well?" Sam stared her down. "What's she got?"

"I don't know yet," Kasia admitted. "I don't know if she has anything for sure."

"Well, I'm sure Junior's boys can figure it out."

"They're just muscle," Kasia objected. "I've worked with them before, Sam. They do their job, but they don't think about it. Not like I do. They can't find their way out of a paper bag without someone to lead them."

Sam made an aggravated noise, almost a growl from the back of his throat. "You don't even know for sure if there's something to find."

"But there could be. And then you'd have that information. Not Junior. Not even me. Not to use it, I mean. As far as I'm concerned, you found it out on your own."

Sam chewed on the inside of his cheek. "Let me guess," he said. "If you figure it out, you want into the Purples."

Electricity shot through her at the thought. But she offered a shrug instead. "If I put Harding in your pocket, you can't argue I haven't earned it." She thought she'd proved her worth a hundred times over, even without the Chief. But Kasia wasn't about to push Sam harder than she had to. If she went too far, he'd deny her out of spite. Then it would take weeks to convince him it was his idea in the first place. She'd done this dance before. She tried to take those steps sparingly.

Fortunately, Sam looked thoughtful. "You're not wrong, kid." He lit his cigarette, took a long inhale, and blew the smoke through his nose. It pooled between them. Kasia knew better than to interrupt him when he was making up his mind. She sat poised, waiting. "Alright. I'll get you the delivery from Junior. But if you're wrong, you're going to find a way to make the trouble worth my time."

That could mean anything from unpaid work to roughing up business owners behind on the cut they owed to the Purples. Unpleasant, but worth the risk. "Thanks, Sam. I owe you if I'm wrong. But I'm not wrong." She flashed a cheeky grin, and Sam chuckled.

"I'm counting on you, Andrew. Don't let me down."

\* \* \*

A WEEK LATER, Kasia was officially in charge of supplying the Lavender with their liquor orders. They'd been told to pack bottles from the Purples carefully in crates meant to supply reams of newsprint paper, and when they got there, Kasia could see why. The alley had a door leading to an open room with a half-dozen people inside, all with ink-stained fingers. Machinery and drafting tables were crammed together with hardly any room between them, a printing press taking up most of the far wall. Newspapers blazoned with the name *The Detroit Worker* were tied with string and stacked haphazardly. A union paper, maybe, or a political group. Someone pointed her toward the basement entrance, a hatch open in the floor in the corner.

She helped carry a box down. The basement was larger than the room they'd come from, spanning maybe half the building. It had been kitted out nicely with a swooping wood bar and a raised platform for performances. A handful of tables filled the space, except about twenty feet right in front of the stage—probably reserved for dancing. James was waiting for them behind the bar. In a brighter light than when they'd met, Kasia noticed he looked distinguished, even casually dressed. His aquiline nose and grey-streaked hair lent him an air of dignity and seriousness she hadn't noticed before. Kasia approached him, hand extended. "James Patrick?"

The man took her hand and shook it firmly. "Good to see you again. Andrew Kasinksi?"

"Kasowski. You can call me Andy. This is Stan and Henry." She hooked a thumb over her shoulder at her friends behind her. "Where do you want the boxes?"

James pointed to the expanse between the end of the bar and the stage. "Right here, I suppose."

"Sure thing. Stan and Henry will bring your order in as soon as we've handled payment."

"Oh. Of course," James said, surprised by what seemed to Kasia like standard business. "Sophia handles the money, and she got tied up with something today. I think she left cash somewhere."

Stan cackled. "You've got a woman handling your money? Better hope she keeps it in the business instead of spending it all on new shoes." Kasia shot him a withering glare, and Stan shrank back.

James gestured for Kasia to follow him. Kasia told her friends to wait and trailed James to a door behind the stage. The room behind it was small, with beaten couches and mirrors lining the walls. He led Kasia through another door into a room that was little more than a storage closet, shelves crammed with boxes, books, and cleaning supplies, with a desk in the middle that made actually retrieving anything unnecessarily dangerous.

James slid between the desk and the shelves, opening drawers and rifling through them. "It's here somewhere." Despite his collected appearance, Kasia thought she heard a tinge of fear in his voice. It satisfied her. Much easier than the customers who thought they could pull one over on her.

"Take your time," she said, magnanimous. Kasia leaned against the wall, her arms crossed. "Sophia won't be in today?"

"Not until tonight." Unsuccessful in his hunt through the drawers, James started lifting stacks of paper. "I'll be right back," he said. "Let me check someplace else."

He left Kasia alone in the cramped office. Kasia felt her neck prickle almost before the idea formed. With a glance over her shoulder, Kasia started thumbing through the papers on the desk. Most of it was useless. If Sophia had an organizational system, Kasia couldn't tell what it was. Personal correspondence mixed with receipts and orders. Catalogues for clothing and housewares nestled in between.

Finally, an address caught her eye, written out in neat script on an empty envelope stuffed into a magazine. *Sophia Worley*. East Ferry Street.

She stuffed the envelope into her pocket just as James reentered the office. "I'm afraid I can't find your payment," he admitted, eyes huge despite his deep-set brows.

Kasia smiled reassuringly. For once, she wasn't mad about a snag keeping her from her money. It gave her an excuse to come back, hopefully while Sophia was around. "As a one-time favor—a show of appreciation for your business—we'll leave the liquor so my colleagues don't have to come back tonight. I'll come in by myself to collect payment. With a 10% late payment fee." She had a reputation to maintain. "I don't think I have to tell you how I'd feel if my generosity were taken advantage of. Or what I might do with those feelings. Doctors these days are saying it's not good to hold them in."

James's anxiety clearly wasn't relieved by the compromise, but he nodded. "Yes, of course. Thank you. I'm sure Sophia will have your payment in full tonight. The password you'll need for entrance is 'boiler.'"

Kasia tipped her hat. "Pleasure doing business with you." She walked him back to the bar with a hand on his shoulder. Kasia motioned for Stan and Henry to put down the boxes and go get the rest from the trunk. She turned to follow them, but then turned back. "When can I expect her to arrive?"

"Sometime around ten, I think."

"Is that when you open?"

"We open at nine. She said to expect her to be fashionably late tonight."

"At ten, then. Thanks for your help, James." Kasia grinned.

Stan grumbled behind her. "I'm not coming back tonight, boss," Stan said. "I've got tickets for my girl and I to see the circus."

"You'll fit right in," Henry said, setting his box down carefully.

"No one needs to come tonight," Kasia said. "I've got it handled." Henry nodded and Stan's shoulders fell in relief. "Let me help with the boxes."

* * *

Kasia told herself she'd wait to talk to Sophia at the club that night. But she couldn't help herself, not with Sophia's address rattling around in her head, temptation growing every minute. After finishing their route, Kasia found the house on East Ferry Street, in the already-dark early evening. It was smaller than some of the other houses, but well-kept. Brick, two stories, with an elegant turret and a bare porch by the front door. The moneyed neighborhood made Kasia squirm. Her perfectly tailored suit suddenly felt shabby. She imagined people looking through their expensive lace curtains at her, certain she was there to rob them.

But she'd done too much work finding Sophia to back

out now. Besides, sometimes getting information was easier than she expected. Plenty of people just needed a little cash motivation. If Sophia was starting a club, she could probably use the money. Kasia learned long ago that sometimes just asking, and offering an incentive for the answer, was a good place to start. She straightened her lapels, jogged up the freshly swept steps, and knocked on the imposing red door.

A woman in a prim black dress answered. She was older than Kasia—maybe in her mid-forties—with streaks of grey in her blonde hair. Kasia thought she was pretty under her stern expression. "May I help you?"

Kasia cleared her throat. "I'm here to see Sophia Worley."

The maid raised an eyebrow. "And you are?"

"Andrew Kasowski," Kasia replied.

"I see." The maid lifted a book from a table next to the door, holding it at an angle so that Kasia couldn't see the pages. "Mr. Kasowski, I don't believe you have an appointment."

Kasia tried to look friendly. Her sharp face and hooded eyes tended to give her an intimidating countenance. Appearing threatening while showing up unannounced didn't seem wise. "Oh, no—I just dropped in for a chat. I'm a new business associate."

"You'll still need an appointment," the maid replied firmly, flipping through the pages. "The next time she's available is in three weeks. Thursday, March 14, at 4:30 pm. However, if you'd like to wait another week...."

"No." Kasia rolled her shoulders, agitation knotting the muscles around her spine. "I don't want to wait three weeks. It's a simple conversation."

"I'm sure, Mr. Kasowski, but you still need an appointment. Ms. Worley has many demands on her time and is on a very strict schedule. I'm sure you understand. Now, do you want the 4:30 appointment on March 14<sup>th</sup>?"

Kasia gripped the door frame, her knuckles turning white. "Look, I didn't want to have to do this," she hissed, leaning in, "but I'm *Andrew Kasowski*. From the Hamtramck Gang. We work under Sam Periera of the Purple Gang." Her name might not be widespread outside of certain circles, but everyone knew Sam.

"Hmm." The maid was remarkably unimpressed. "Yes, I see. Does that mean you do or do not want the appointment at 4:30 on March 14<sup>th</sup>?"

Kasia thought very hard about simply shouldering open the door, walking past this annoying woman, and finding Sophia herself. As if she could sense her intentions—or maybe she was just bored waiting for an answer—the maid began to close the door on her. Kasia hastily pushed back. "Wait, wait, wait. Alright. 4:30 on March 14<sup>th</sup>."

The other woman nodded, noted it in the schedule, and placed the book back on the table. "Very well. We'll see you at 4:30 on March 14<sup>th</sup>, Mr. Kasowski." Before Kasia could respond, the maid closed the door. She stood for a moment, staring at the metal numbers screwed into the wood, unsure if she felt more defeated or annoyed.

She retreated across the street and lit a cigarette, gathering herself. A gorgeous new Ford Model A pulled around the corner and came to a stop in front of Sophia's house. Kasia watched, curious to see who would come out of the car. Instead it idled, waiting.

Sophia appeared on her porch. Unlike the other night, her dress was tailored to her natural waist. The black silk brought out the lush curves of her hourglass figure, even beneath the unbuttoned fur-lined coat she'd thrown on top of it. For a moment, Kasia lost her breath. She could feel her heartbeat in her throat. Kasia told herself it was because the dress was more appealing than the trendy boyish silhouettes favored by flappers; Sophia offered something different, something impossibly luscious and ripe. Her fingers twitched around her cigarette. She couldn't help wonder what the lustrous fabric would feel like in her hands while lifting the dress, freeing Sophia's stockinged legs inch by inch until the tender flesh of her thighs appeared. Kasia inhaled sharply, trying to push aside the thought, as she watched Sophia stride towards the car.

An impulse tugged Kasia forward. It wasn't in the plan. After she was rejected at Sophia's door, she'd fully intended just to watch the house for a minute. But without a single thought to counter it, the auto's door closed behind Sophia, and Kasia sprinted across the street. She flung the door open and slid in next to the other woman, the two now only inches from each other in the back seat.

Kasia's eyes widened. She pressed herself against the door, as if she wasn't the one who'd jumped into a stranger's car. *Shit. Now what do I do?*

"Oh!" Sophia pushed away, putting as much distance between them as she could. "What on earth do you think you're doing?" Her voice, deep and as smooth as a rock pulled from the lake, contrasted beautifully with the driver's frantic yelling for her to get out. Kasia wanted to sink into the warmth of it.

"I'm, uh—Andrew Kasowski," Kasia said, dodging a blow coming from the driver in the front seat. *What do I even say?* "I just want to talk to you."

"You can make an appointment, then," said Sophia. "I'm not inclined to chat with men who accost me in my own car."

The driver was getting out of the front seat. As awkward as she felt, Kasia knew she had to work fast. *Harding. You're here for information about Harding.* "It's not that kind of talk. I just want some information from you." The door behind her swung open, and the driver grabbed her waist. She braced herself against the seat, hanging on for dear life. "Just give me a few minutes to ask you some questions," she said, her voice strained as the man's arm dug into her stomach. "Just a few minutes, and I'll be out of your hair for good. You won't have to see me again." That *was* a lie. She planned on picking up every payment from Sophia herself.

Sophia studied her carefully. Somehow, her nervous expression hardened into stubborn acceptance. Kasia hadn't thought her argument was good, but maybe she'd caught her curiosity. "I run the beverage delivery service for your club," she admitted. "I work for Sam." *Maybe I should have led with that.*

Sophia gestured to the driver behind Kasia. "Robert," she said, and the man stopped pulling. "Mr. Kasowski can stay." She gave Kasia a pointed look. "For now."

Kasia took a deep breath as the driver's arm left her waist. He shot her a dirty look as he closed the door behind him and returned to the front seat. Sophia was smoothing her finger-waved hair. "You have roughly five minutes before I'm at my destination, Mr. Kasowski. If I were you, I'd make good use of them."

Sophia's closeness—so close that Kasia could see the sweep of blush over her cheeks, the pins holding back her hair, the golden rings around her pupils—threw every intention she'd had out of Kasia's brain. Her mouth opened and closed as she tried to remember what she was there for. She finally collected herself enough to say the only thing that came to mind. "You owe me money for your delivery today."

Sophia's eyes widened in disbelief. "So you accosted me in my car?"

"No. Well, yes," Kasia said. Her confidence deflated further, pierced under Sophia's glaring green eyes. "Payment is due on delivery." Kasia took a breath, finally gathering herself. "But I'll waive the penalty if you help me out. I saw you at the police station last week. I know you have a relationship with the police chief."

There was a confused pause. Sophia laughed. "Relationship?"

"I don't know what kind of relationship," Kasia admitted. "But I want to know. I'd make it worth your time."

Sophia cracked a window and lit a cigarette, the air fluttering the fur collar of her jacket. "And why, exactly, are you interested?"

"The Purple Gang doesn't have Harding in their pocket. But you do. I want to know why."

Sophia lifted and dropped her elegant shoulders. "I'm a friend of the family," she said.

Kasia's brows furrowed. "How did you become friends with the Harding family?"

The woman shrugged again. "I'm friends with all kinds of people."

Kasia pulled her wallet out of her inner coat pocket, counted out ten dollars, and set it on the seat between them. "I said I'd make it worth your time. How did you become friends with the Harding family?"

Sophia took a long look at the cash, then pushed it back towards Kasia with one manicured finger. "You don't seem to know what my time is worth, Mr. Kasowski."

Kasia frowned. She pulled another ten out of her wallet

and added it to the pile. "I'm doing you a favor," she insisted. "Sam has an idea of what you've got going for you with Harding. He'll want to know more. And he won't be nearly as nice about it as I am. Do you catch my drift?"

Sophia took a drag from her cigarette, blowing the smoke in a stream out the window. "He'll be as disappointed as you, then. There's no amount of money Sam can offer me to talk about the chief. I'd rather he dump me in the lake, if it came down to it." She put out the cigarette in the built-in ashtray between them. "Now, if there's nothing else, you can get out at the next corner." She tossed her hair and turned toward the window. The cold shoulder looked regal on Sophia.

It wasn't going well, but Kasia couldn't waste the opportunity completely. She pushed the $20 back toward the other woman. "Take it. For the intrusion," she said. It earned her a glance from the corner of Sophia's eyes. Kasia was embarrassed by how much a single, dismissive glare from Sophia made her stomach flip. "You can give it back to me later. When you pay me tonight for delivery. And another ten percent."

The driver parked on the corner and turned to Kasia, still furious. "*Out*," he demanded.

Kasia did as she was told, holding the door open for a moment to look at Sophia. Seeming to feel her gaze, the woman turned towards her. Her face looked as though it was carved from marble. Kasia's grip on the door tightened. She felt as though she'd crawl over broken glass just for one glance from Sophia, and three times over for a single word. "Five percent," Sophia said.

Kasia's face fell. Apparently, the one thing that could break the spell Sophia put on her was bargaining. "Ten," Kasia said tersely. She slammed the door shut.

# Chapter Nine

When Kasia returned to the Lavender, one lone man was running the printing press in the office above it. His sleepy eyes turned to Kasia; he stretched like a cat being woken up from a nap. "Can I help you?"

"You can," Kasia said. "I'm here to check the boiler."

The man nodded and opened the hatch to the basement. "Right this way." The sound of a band playing a swinging jazz rhythm swirled up from below.

Kasia tilted her chin up in thanks and descended the steps. It was only ten, but the bar was busy. People clustered together in little packs. A few couples—mostly men with men and women with women—danced together in front of the stage. James was behind the bar again, this time pouring drinks for the crowd on the other side. Kasia approached, and wedged herself in between two people, ignoring the indignant "Hey!" from a woman beside her. "Sophia here yet?" She had to raise her voice to be heard over the music.

James glanced at her, freezing for a moment, before answering. "She's in the back. She'll be out in a minute."

Her eyes swept the room until it landed on the door tucked behind the stage. She settled in nearby, watching the band. A few minutes later, the door swung open. Sophia appeared. She'd changed into a deep emerald green dress, with feathers adorning her finger-waved hair. Kasia immediately noticed how the color brought out her eyes.

Sophia saw her right away, cocking her head and flashing Kasia a look of annoyance that almost withered her. Given her line of work (and the first impression she'd left) she didn't expect a warm welcome. But Sophia's fearlessness cut her off at the knees. As she approached, Sophia gathered herself, and her expression shifted back into haughty mischievousness. "Thank you for showing up in the *appropriate* place to collect your payment, Mr. Kasowski," she said. The lightness of her tone didn't soften her. She placed her hands on her hips, the motion tucking her dress further around the curve of her waist. "I don't know what you've been taught, but women don't appreciate being followed by a man like a stray dog."

The insult should have offended Kasia, but instead she felt hot embarrassment rise under her collar. She shoved it aside, letting indignation cover it. "I'm not in the habit of sitting back and waiting to be paid, whether or not you think that makes me a dog."

Sophia huffed through her nostrils and tossed her head —for all the world like a horse in high spirits, if they were going to really lean in on the animal comparisons, Kasia thought. "Fine. Come with me."

Sophia led her into the room behind the stage. The band had left the couches covered in instrument cases and sheet music. She opened the office, hip-checked the desk a few inches forward and squatted behind it, and began pulling boxes from the shelf. Kasia squinted. "Do you need help with that?"

"No." Sophia revealed a safe built into the wall. She shielded the lock from Kasia's sight as she spun the combination. It opened with a soft click. She pulled out a stack of bills, counted them rapidly, and held them out to Kasia. "There."

Kasia counted it herself, then tapped the stack against her palm. "You're missing ten percent."

Sophia closed the safe hard, with a metallic clang, and stood. She was short, even in heels, but while her head craned up to look at Kasia, the fierceness of Sophia's gaze made her feel like they stood eye-to-eye. "Payment isn't late. It's been made the same day as delivery."

Kasia frowned. "That's cute, but payment is due at *time of* delivery. And if there's one thing I know about Sam, it's that he's very clear about his contracts." She leaned against the desk, propping one foot casually behind the other. "It's only fair for everyone to be clear about expectations. Right?" She drummed her fingers against the desktop. "Of course, if you don't like the terms of the contract, you can operate a dry bar. Maybe turn it into a coffeehouse."

Sophia glared, and Kasia knew she had her. There was no other liquor supplier in town. The Purple Gang was it. Slowly, Sophia squatted back down and opened the safe again. She counted out another, smaller stack of bills, and threw it on the desk next to Kasia's hand. With the safe closed and the boxes moved back in place, she stood. "There, Mr. Kasowski. You got what you came for." She eyed Kasia, a knowing smile forming. "Unless you didn't?" She tilted her head towards the club's main room. "Maybe you want to hang around... see what we're about." Sophia's eyes slid down Kasia's form and back up, taking her in. "You might enjoy spending time with people who don't judge what you are... or what you like."

Kasia's heart dropped to her feet. Sophia had seen through her, straight into her deepest fear. She felt like she was choking. Kasia cleared her throat and stepped back quickly. "No, no." She tugged at her jacket. "I won't take up any more of your time." She lifted her hat. "Goodnight, Ms. Worley."

She fled back out of the room, up the stairs, into the frigid night. Kasia imagined Sophia laughing behind her. It echoed soundlessly in her ears. She hated to admit it. She fled nothing. But what that was, she thought as she took deep breaths that sent plumes of white fog streaming behind her as she walked, was fleeing.

Sophia knew. And that meant Sophia scared the shit out of her.

# Chapter Ten

"Andrew. Three men here to see you." Czeslaw's voice was quick and tense. "Cops."

Kasia's eyes shot up from the ledger on her desk in the paper supply's warehouse. "What do they want?"

Czeslaw shook his head. "They wouldn't say. But they know your name, and they know you're here."

Kasia closed the book hard, sending dust flying. "Take this." She shoved the ledger into Czeslaw's hands. "Do they have anyone out back?"

"I don't know. Maybe."

"Then put it in the cellar. You know what to do. Hide anything that needs hiding." Czeslaw nodded and starting pushing heavy boxes of paper aside to expose the cellar door. "I'll try to keep them up front until you're done." Kasia pulled another ledger from the desk drawer, this one full of the paper supply's transactions, and set it out as if she'd been working on it instead. With a deep, steady breath, Kasia settled her face into an expression of mild inconvenience. She knew this was always a possibility, but she wouldn't pay the piper his debt without a fight.

It wasn't just cops standing in the front office of the warehouse. It was Chief Harding himself, flanked by two uniformed officers. Fear gripped Kasia's throat. She forced herself to extend a hand. "Andrew Kasowski."

The Chief took her hand, pumping it in a firm two shakes. "Police Chief Richard Harding. This is Officer Brown and Officer Christianson."

Kasia raised a brow, head tilted in feigned confusion. "And to what do I owe the pleasure of meeting the Police Chief himself?"

Chief Harding smiled broadly. It didn't reach his narrowed, calculating eyes. "Well, son, I've put together a task force for a cause that's dear to my heart. Normally, I wouldn't be involved in day-to-day operations. But I'm a former detective—a damn good one, if I do say so myself— and sometimes... something comes along that makes the ol' itch demand to be scratched. Sometimes you get promoted out of the work you love best. I'm happy to say that I've got an exception to come back out in the field."

He liked to hear himself talk. That much was clear. "And what does that have to do with me?" Kasia asked.

The Chief took off his hat and slicked back his greased hair. His gray streaks shone brightly in the office lights. "I'm glad you asked, son. I'm hoping you can help me understand a few things. You see, when I work on a case, I have a way of getting hung up on little details. Things that don't quite make sense to me. I have to put these details to bed in order to move forward. You can answer those questions for me, and I'll be out of your hair."

Kasia's hands gripped into fists by her side. She forced herself to relax her fingers. "Questions about what, sir?"

Chief Harding's easy demeanor tensed, just a little. A dog grabbing a bone. "You've been seen with Sam Periera. But you're not from his neighborhood, are you, Andrew? You've got no natural connection to him as far as I can tell. You're too young to be school buddies and you're not family friends. I've noticed that Sam doesn't like to hang around with anyone outside his people. So, I got to thinking." The Chief tapped the pleated dome of his hat with one finger. "How did a Polish kid from Hamtramck meet a closed-off guy like Sam?"

"Business. He gets his ledgers and invoices from us. Goes through a lot." The Purple Gang ran plenty of legitimate businesses to launder bootlegging money. They needed paper like everyone else.

"That so?" Chief Harding said. "And the paper supply's accountant delivers them personally? That's good service." He frowned and shook a pointed finger, still holding his hat. "But I still don't get it. You sit with him and talk about what, ledgers?"

Kasia shrugged. "He took a liking to me. He's got a son about my age. Likes to offer advice. Bit of a mentor. He saw I was struggling when I came back from the war."

"Ah, right. The 32$^{nd}$ Infantry Division, wasn't it? You were listed as missing in action during Meuse-Argonne. Then you show back up here," he gestured to Kasia, "all in one piece, I see. Like you rose from the dead. Good for you, son. Good for you. Too many of our boys never made it back. Especially since you're your mother's only son. Surprising, really. You people breed like rabbits." There was a flash of disdain in Harding's eyes. He waited for Kasia to fight him on the comment, like she was in any position to defend herself. But she'd heard every opinion there was to hear about the Polish. She wasn't about to cede ground to an asshole. When she didn't respond, he continued. "Tell me, where were you all that time in between?"

Kasia's nails dug trenches into her palm. "Head injury from an explosion. Shellshock too. Didn't even know who I was. Can't remember how I ended up in a private hospital. Took a long time to recover. All I knew when I did was that I wanted to come back home."

"That's quite a story." The Chief pulled a face of insincere sympathy. "You've been through a lot, son. It must've moved Sam real deep to hear it."

"Yes, sir."

"And what kind of mentorship does Sam provide?"

"Oh, you know. Keep your nose clean. Don't get hung up with women or liquor. Stay away from the ponies. Tries to keep me on the straight and narrow."

"Good advice. Never known a Pole who could keep it." The Chief placed his hat carefully back on his head.

"Anything else I can help you with?" Kasia's voice came out sharper than she intended.

"Not at the moment, Andrew. I appreciate your candor. Do me a favor and don't go out of town anytime soon, eh? Never know when a few more questions might pop up."

"Alright." Kasia watched them leave. Harding stopped at the door to tip his hat. She didn't relax until she watched him round the corner, out of sight.

# Chapter Eleven

"Well? Did you find out what you needed to?" Sam asked as soon as Kasia sat in the booth across from him. She'd been surprised Sam still wanted to meet at the deli, despite her warning about the man across the street. Maybe he figured he'd be watched anywhere.

"No," Kasia answered. Sam frowned. But Kasia wasn't in the habit of making excuses.

"Why not?" Sam said.

"I offered her twenty dollars. She said she couldn't be bought." Kasia pulled out a cigarette, careful to keep the pack in her pocket to avoid riling Sam further.

"Everyone can be bought."

"Yeah, yeah. Find her price." Kasia lit her cigarette and tilted her head back, letting the smoke spill out into the air from her open mouth. "My pockets aren't bottomless."

"You're asking me for money?" Sam said.

"No." Kasia rested her elbow on the table. "She doesn't want money."

"Then what does she want?"

"I don't know, Sam." Kasia risked a glare. "But I'm going to find out."

"How?"

"I'll figure it out."

Sam rubbed his forehead. "What do you mean, figure it out? If she won't cooperate, force it out of her. Corner her, rough her up until she talks. You want leverage against Harding, or a date? Don't be a gentleman. It's getting in the way of my money."

A chill pierced Kasia. She tensed, lower lip between her teeth, like she was bracing against wind whipping off the lake. She thought of what she'd told Sophia about Sam being less patient than her. "I'm not sure if she has the connection I thought she did." It was a flat-out lie. And no one lied to Sam Pereira. She could have told him what she knew, however little it was, and he'd send someone to find out the rest. She told herself that she was stalling for time. Even if it meant taking Sam's wrath.

Sam looked unconvinced. "Suddenly you don't know? I stuck my neck out for you with this."

"I just don't want to bring you bad info. You know how it is. I'm trying to separate the rumors from the facts."

Sam snorted. "You chasing skirt?"

"What?" Kasia felt it like a blow to her cheek. "You think I'm playing you for pussy?"

"You wouldn't be the first guy, Andrew." Sam looked weary, the anger leaving him. "I just didn't expect it from you."

It was worse than the fury she'd anticipated. "I'm not chasing skirt, Sam." She shifted in her seat, leaning in. "Look, just give me some time. I know what to do." It was another lie. She didn't like the risks she was taking.

Sam snorted again. If anything, he looked more deeply suspicious. "Where's my money for the week?"

Kasia pulled the envelope from her jacket and dropped it in front of him. She watched him look over his shoulder before counting the bills inside. She'd shaken his trust already. It didn't bode well. "One more thing," Kasia said.

"What's that?" Sam barely glanced up at her.

"The chief came by the office."

Sam stopped counting. "Oh yeah? And what'd he say?"

"He knows we're connected. And about my... service in the war." Kasia remembered the other paper bag in her coat. She set it in front of Sam. "I deliver you ledgers."

Sam picked the bag up and looked inside. "Ledgers? That's what you came up with?"

"You like me because I remind you of your son. And they're nice ledgers."

Sam threw the bag back down. "You know what I'm going to say, right?"

Kasia nodded. "Get the info—"

Sam spoke the rest of the sentence with her. "—The information you need from Sophia Worley."

"Got it," Kasia said. Sam dismissed her with a wave and a grunt.

# Chapter Twelve

Sam's accusation felt like a wool jacket worn against bare skin. It was itchy and hot, but she couldn't take it off and run her nails over her arms until the feeling went away. It made sleep impossible. She spent the night rolling around in her bed, each turn more uncomfortable than the last. *You chasing skirt?* Sam's question repeated in her mind, more aggravating each time it came back around. She'd prioritized Sam's business for a decade. So she'd opted for a softer touch than usual—did that give him a right to question her loyalty?

*That's business, kid.* She could hear Sam say it. Not that day, but a hundred times before. Any time someone questioned his decisions or methods. By the time the room turned gray with the first dawn light, she realized Sam was right. It *was* business. If she had to prove herself to him again, she'd do it.

She knew how Sam would handle Sophia. If it were up to him, he'd threaten Sophia's liquor delivery if she didn't tell him what she knew about Chief Harding. He might send some goons down to the Lavender to cause a little trouble—broken glasses, smashed chairs. If that didn't work, he'd start threatening knees with baseball bats and property with bullet holes. Sophia said she'd rather force Sam to dump her in the river than give up what she knew. Kasia didn't know if she realized how real the threat of that was.

But Kasia wasn't Sam. Not that she typically favored a subtler approach; Sam's methods were tried and true. They'd served her well more than once. She just didn't think they were necessary. Not yet. She had other options. Maybe it was Sophia's proximity to Kasia's secret, but she couldn't bear the thought of using the same methods on her that she would on anyone else. She'd get what she needed from Sophia and prove herself to Sam her own way.

First things first. If Sophia was so busy, Kasia wanted to know what she was doing.

For three days, Kasia sent Henry and Stan in shifts to scope out Sophia's house. It was a residential street, making a lingerer or a parked paper van suspicious. After making Henry dress Stan so he didn't look so disheveled, she had them each walk the street like a gentleman on a turn around the neighborhood.

"There's nothing to see," Stan complained when he got back to the warehouse after his third stakeout. He ran a gloved hand over his leaking red nose. "She has friends over regularly. Big deal."

Kasia threw a paper down in front of him, folded over to display a photo of Chief Harding and his wife. "Any of them look like this?"

"No. They're all women."

Kasia tapped the photo. "Stan. Are any of them *this* woman?" She tried to keep the exasperation out of her voice.

Stan looked miserable, rubbing the cold off his cheeks. "I don't think so."

Kasia turned to Henry, sitting on a couch with a book in his hands. "What about you, you recognize her?"

Henry stood and stretched before ambling over to Kasia's desk. He glanced down. "Nope. Haven't seen her. I did see a man, though. Tall, graying temples. Handsome. Deep tan. Looked sort of trim and sporty, like he spends a lot of time playing tennis."

Kasia sighed, almost certain Henry had just described James. "Have you identified *any* of her visitors?" She had more faith in Henry's work than Stan's.

Henry shrugged. "A few. Society ladies." He pulled a piece of paper from his pocket. "Loretta Johnson. Kitty Davis. Evelyn Watson. Betty Fredericks."

"See if you can connect any of them to Harding," Kasia said. She pulled on her coat and hat.

"Are we doing deliveries already?" Stan complained. "I just walked all the way back here. I'm freezing my ass off."

"I told you I'd throw you an extra couple dollars for your trouble." Kasia pulled cash out of her pocket and handed bills to each of her friends. "That warm you up at all?"

"Thanks, boss," Henry said before Stan could respond. He nudged Stan with his elbow. "Come on. The sooner we get the work done, the sooner you can get back to your girl. Bet she knows a few ways to keep you warm."

Stan looked dreamy for a moment. He eventually shook his head, coming back to earth. "Alright, alright. Let's get a move on." Henry clapped a hand over his shoulder.

\* \* \*

IF SHE WANTED something done right, Kasia thought, she might as well do it herself. She tried to ignore that the possibility of seeing Sophia—at a safe distance, where she couldn't make observations about Kasia's proclivities—made her stomach churn and her heart pound. She sent Stan and Henry on their deliveries alone the next day. Not long after sunrise, she put her plan into motion.

The neighborhood grocer had a truck and owed Kasia a favor. She only had to remind him she'd gotten his money back after a robbery a couple of years ago. After the suspects turned up to church the next day with broken arms and bloodshot eyes, he could practically leave the door wide open at night. What was the big deal about taking his truck out for an afternoon spin in return? The grocer, a reasonable man, handed over the keys.

She parked a few houses down from Sophia, a month of the paper's society pages stacked on the seat next to her. Kasia watched the windows for any sign of movement inside. It made her antsy, thinking of Sophia behind the glass. She pictured her at a vanity, spreading color over her lips, running a comb through her hair. Sophia's pouting mouth, morning light caressing the pale length of her neck. The imagined intimacy made Kasia's stomach clench. She slumped down in her seat and lit a cigarette, shoving the image out of her head.

It didn't take long for boredom to set in. Kasia hated sitting still. She'd never been good at it. Her back stiffened from the car's hard bench seat. She considered getting out to stretch, but a woman walking by with some kind of tiny long-haired spaniel kept her in place.

An hour went by before a car pulled up to the curb. Kasia leaned forward, squinting through the windshield. A woman walked to Sophia's door. Petite, blonde, a little ski-slope nose. The maid answered, and the woman disappeared inside. Kasia thumbed through the papers beside her until she found a likely match. Kitty Davis. She circled the photo with a pen.

An interminable two hours of nothing followed. Itching for something to do, Kasia resorted to smoking one cigarette after the other and watching the shadows move with the sun. When the door finally opened, Sophia was escorting Kitty. Kasia ducked down and watched the women exchange goodbyes, kissing each other's cheeks. Sophia was in a blue day dress with a sailor's collar tied in a neat point against her chest. Kasia wondered what the brush of her lips felt like against Kitty's cheek. She flushed, her chest tightening. Envy churned her stomach. The door closed. Kitty walked to her waiting car.

An hour later, another car carrying another woman parked in front of Sophia's house. The same lackluster scene as before played out in front of Kasia. She was starting to understand Stan's frustration. Kasia decided to find a bakery for breakfast and grab the day's newspaper to add to her pile. When she got back to Sophia's, the woman was leaving. Kasia sighed and settled back in her seat. She checked her watch. Seven or eight hours before Sophia would leave for the Lavender. It was going to be a long day.

# Chapter Thirteen

Kasia woke the next morning when her back, tight and angry, belatedly protested the hours she spent in the car. It felt like the muscles running along her spine curled into themselves before exploding into flame. She groaned into her pillow. Somehow, the frustration churning in her chest was worse than the pain in her back.

Nothing. That's what she'd gathered from her time watching Sophia. The two women came and went. Then hours of even more nothing, not a twitch of a curtain, while Kasia grew more and more impatient. Between Henry and Stan's vigils and her own, all she knew was that Sophia had a busy social schedule. So she knew a bunch of other wealthy women. So what? What did that tell Kasia that she didn't already know? She'd keep Stan and Henry on it for a few more days. But there was only so much surveillance they could do before they made the neighbors suspicious.

She shuffled to the warehouse through the cold. Sitting at her desk was so uncomfortable that she promptly gave up and stretched out on the couch instead. Flopping back against the cushions sent spiraling clouds of dust into the air. Kasia sighed and threw an arm over her eyes.

The pain made her broody. Sophia wouldn't be bribed, and spying on her private life hadn't worked. Kasia felt like she was panning for gold and getting only rocks. She remembered what Sam said: *force it out of her.* It made her stomach sink. Kasia didn't particularly want to rough up a woman in the first place. What's more, something about Sophia made it unthinkable. Kasia snorted, the sound creating a faint echo against the warehouse's high walls. She was getting soft. Letting her feelings get in the way of good business.

Maybe in more ways than one. The thought shot through her. She'd been so thrown by Sophia's willingness to be open in ways that she wasn't, Kasia had assumed that her public life would be barren of any clues about her secret. It wasn't logical. It was a feeling. A vague impression that nothing could hide with a spotlight on it. But how often did people get too comfortable in the warmth of their reputation and end up telling on themselves, at least a little? Surprisingly often, in Kasia's experience.

Sophia hadn't left her house much except to go to the Lavender. But the club was new; maybe once things were settled, she'd head somewhere else, with Stan and Henry following. Once Kasia had that information, she could talk to some of Sophia's friends and acquaintances. Kasia thought it over before heaving a sigh. It was a gamble, and not one that felt like a winner. Who knew how long it would take before Sophia felt comfortable spending her time away from her business? She'd also have to do it without alerting Sophia, giving her time to tie up any loose ends. If she wasn't already after Kasia confronted her.

*Make the spotlight work for you,* Kasia thought. What if

she got in close to Sophia—right in front of her? Get to know her. Watch who she spoke to. Ask a few subtle questions out in the open. Figure out who might be willing to talk in private.

Closeness to Sophia. It scared the fuck out of her. The thought alone made her nauseous. But there was also a pull in her chest—an ache, an instinct. Drawing near her felt right. Kasia trusted her gut. It had steered her well so far—to the top of her game, Sam's best contractor. If she wasn't going to let feelings get in the way, she couldn't let fear drive her.

Just as she'd convinced herself of the plan, the door to the warehouse swung open with a harsh squeal. Czeslaw's voice followed. "You, uh... alright, boss?"

Kasia dropped her arm. Czeslaw's face loomed over her, brows furrowed. Kasia sighed. Czeslaw coming in and interrupting her thoughts wasn't unusual. The Hamtramck Gang operated out of his family business, after all, and he worked for both. He didn't need the money—that was just Czeslaw. A family man. She sometimes found his closeness with them grating. It magnified her mother's distance. But she couldn't fault his work ethic or his careful attention to the people he loved.

She rubbed her face, trying to pull her attention back from the warring feelings she was already tired of managing. "Yeah. I'm fine. What do you need?"

"Sam's on the phone for you," Czeslaw said.

Kasia shot up and winced when her back protested the sudden movement. Sam rarely called. He preferred in-person conversations, without the risk of an eavesdropping operator. Her shoulders, already in knots, somehow tightened more. She nearly ran to the front office, where Czeslaw's aunt held the receiver and mouthpiece with a disapproving frown. Housing the gang headquarters was deviant enough in the woman's eyes, tolerated only for the rental income Kasia provided. A Purple calling was clearly beyond what decorum could tolerate. Kasia offered an apologetic look as she took the phone. "Sam?"

Sam didn't bother with a greeting. "I need you to talk to a guy."

Kasia turned her back towards Czeslaw and his aunt, keeping her voice low. "Who?"

"A business owner. He has some concerns about joining the neighborhood business association." Kasia knew he meant the Purple's protection racket. Collecting money for the "safety" of the business—from the Purples, who would destroy it without a mandatory incentive. She'd been sent to meet with business owners that didn't want to buy in before. That was years ago, when she was young, hungry, and had to prove herself to Sam. She'd always hated it. It made her feel sick. She'd refused to set up the same con on her own turf. Grateful neighbors seemed better for business than angry ones, anyway.

"Why me?" Kasia asked. She rarely pushed back against a direct order, but this one made her uneasy. "Don't you have guys to handle neighborhood relations?"

Sam raised his voice. "Because I told you to. You need to remember how business works, Andrew. You need to prove to me you've still got your head in the game. Besides, you owe me a favor."

Her boss never forgot a debt. And Kasia knew she owed him one after he got the Lavender on her delivery route. She hoped she'd have more time to pay him back with the information about Harding he wanted. Clearly, Sam wasn't waiting around.

She'd been silent for too long. "Well?" Sam said. "Can I count on you or not?"

"Yeah. Yeah, of course." Kasia wanted nothing more than to crawl back to the couch, stare at the ceiling, and avoid the whole project. But this was Sam. Everything she had depended on his good will. "You can always count on me."

"Good." The smugness in Sam's voice rankled Kasia's nerves. "I'll give you the address."

* * *

KASIA DIDN'T LIKE the protection racket. But Joe did. They'd hardly spoken since she'd cut off the tip of his tongue. Joe didn't speak much in general after that. Probably to hide the slight lisp he'd developed. But when she tracked him down in the neighborhood and told him the plan, his eyes lit up.

Joe's good mood was short-lived. It usually was. They'd hardly gotten into the delivery truck when he started complaining. "Why are Stan and Henry getting extra work? I could use the money too, you know."

Kasia leaned against her seat and propped her feet on the dashboard, hoping to relieve the strain on her back. "You *are* getting extra work, Joe. Right now. I'm paying you for it, aren't I?"

"Yeah, for the afternoon. They're getting whole days."

"It's not a task you're suited for, Joe." Her temples were pounding, and Joe's attitude wasn't helping. Kasia pulled her hat over her eyes. The day was overcast, but the sunlight felt piercing to her aching head.

"But those guys are? Henry, sure. But Stan? He's a thick-skulled idiot."

"Stan's not an idiot," Kasia said sharply. "And he's got more patience than you. I barely have enough patience for surveillance. I know you don't." Joe scoffed. She couldn't see him behind her hat, but Kasia could picture his flaring nostrils and red face. It was a common look for him. "You want more money to lose on the ponies, fine. If I see a job you're good at, I'll give it to you. Like I did today. Right now."

A brief, blissful moment of silence raised Kasia's hopes that the conversation was done. But when Joe lost an argument, he just chose a different front to fight on. "Do you know how hard it is running deliveries by myself? What happened to 'no one does a job alone,' from back in the early days, huh?"

Kasia gripped her crossed arms. She fought to keep her voice even. "That was before you drove off any partners, Joe. You complained and bitched and yelled until none of the guys wanted to work with you. I kept you on as a favor. We were kids together. That counts for something. But you make things harder for everyone, and you make things harder for yourself."

"It's not my fault they can't do anything right!" Joe yelled.

The sound rattled Kasia's skull and made her head throb harder. She took her feet off the dashboard and sat up, pulling herself tall in her seat and pushing her hat from her face. "Their work is fine. The problem is you. If you don't want to work alone, learn a little humility. Maybe take a look at the other seven virtues while you're at it."

Joe hit the brakes hard. Kasia had to catch herself to keep from flying into the dashboard. She was about to ask what the fuck Joe thought he was doing when he threw the gear into park and growled, "We're here."

Kasia got out of the truck and adjusted her coat collar, scowling so hard her jaw ached. Then she looked up at the sign on the shop in front of them. Her hand grabbed for something to steady her, but met only the cold, smooth expanse of the truck cab. A candy shop. She'd been sent to intimidate a man who sold candy to children.

Joe marched ahead. If he had any qualms, he didn't show it. Kasia trailed behind, pulling in deep gulps of air.

A bell rang against the door as they entered. A man in his forties, with auburn, slicked-back hair and a spotless white apron, appeared from the back. "Can I help you?"

Joe looked at Kasia. She stepped forward, trying to hide the trepidation that made her want to disappear. "Sam sent us. He'd like you to reconsider joining the neighborhood business association."

The man's face immediately tightened, glowering. "Not a chance in hell, pal. I'm not giving the Purples any of my money."

Joe wandered along the shelves of glass jars holding colorful confections. He paused in front of the Charleston Chews. With one hand behind his back, he used the other to swipe the container to the floor. It shattered, sending flecks of glass flying across his boots. Kasia winced.

The proprietor's face turned an explosive red. "Get out," he yelled, pointing towards the door.

Joe sent another container to the floor. "Oops," he said. "This is nothing though, right? Accidents happen. You build it into your budget, even." He walked to the glass counter, shards crunching under his feet, to overturn a display of lollipops. Kasia opened her mouth, ready to call him off. She bit back the words. They couldn't go back to Sam without completing the job. Joe continued. "The problem is, you can never predict when accidents will happen." He kicked the front of the counter. The glass shattered and collapsed in a sharp, gleaming waterfall. "Too many in a row, and a business can't survive the pressure."

The man stepped closer to the broken counter, face hovering inches from Joe's. "I said get out. You're not getting a damn cent."

Kasia's heart sank. He was brave. She admired it. It made everything harder.

A grin broke across Joe's face. He started chuckling—low at first, then building into a hysterical guffaw. He leaped across the counter, pushing the man back into a row of shelves. The shelves trembled, jars tipping and falling around them. Joe grabbed his arms and pinned them behind his back. Then he looked at Kasia.

Joe's grin was gone, replaced with narrowed, hungry eyes and a sly smirk. Kasia stared back, fighting the chill that overtook her. Joe smelled blood. He smelled weakness. *Her* weakness. Her hesitation. He wasn't being deferential. He was issuing a challenge. Just like Sam had.

Her world didn't look kindly on unanswered challenges. Respect depended on stepping up to the call. Kasia's stomach turned. She wanted to lean over and puke on the broken glass. Instead, she picked her way around the counter, already reaching for the gun in her coat. Kasia paused in front of the candy seller, raising the gun above his head. He stared back, defiant, and spit on her feet.

Kasia swung the gun down, driving the butt into the man's cheek. The impact vibrated through her hand and arm, all the way to her shoulder. She wanted to stop. In her head, she screamed at herself to end this now. But she couldn't. Not with Joe watching her balk.

She rained blows over the man's head, blood coating her hand with each hit. He tried to pull away, screaming like the damned, cuts blooming over his cheeks and forehead. Kasia stopped, breathing heavy and uneven. The man sobbed and slumped against Joe's hold.

Kasia placed the muzzle to his temple and cocked the trigger. *Don't make me do this,* she thought. She wasn't sure if the thought was for the man or herself. She pressed the gun into the thin flesh and hard bone beneath it. "Now that you've had a minute to think, have you changed your mind?" *Please,* she thought. *Please.* Her hand trembled. She prayed Joe couldn't see. A deep inhale steadied her just enough to hide it.

The man nodded, sending a string of blood from his nose to the floor. "Yes," he finally said in a ragged whisper. Kasia stepped back and pointed to the cash register. Joe released him. The man pressed a button and the cash drawer opened. Kasia dug through the change and bills until she'd counted out what Sam was owed.

Joe made a show of brushing the candy seller off, smearing blood farther down his starched white apron. "Pleasure doing business with you," he said. "Welcome to the neighborhood business association."

Hands in his pockets, Joe walked out whistling. The man collapsed, sobs racking his body. Kasia recoiled from the sight. She followed Joe out with her eyes on the floor.

# Chapter Fourteen

Kasia spent the next day in bed. She blamed her back, but the problem was her head. She couldn't stop seeing the man at the candy store —on the floor, blood and snot oozing over his mouth as he sobbed, hands clutching the broken glass around him.

Why did *this* man, *this* job, make her feel so heavy she couldn't fathom facing the world? She'd done it for Sam before. And plenty of other jobs, no less bloody, that never weighed on her mind like this.

Ambition had a way of making the details of how she reached her goal unimportant. Not in the planning—the plan was always detailed. But she did what she had to, and that was that. Every move was a step up the ladder. Omelets required a few broken eggs, or whatever the saying was. She didn't spare the shells much thought. This time, though... she hadn't wanted to do it. Ambition usually distanced her from the process. Where was it now?

The question scratched at a door she didn't want to open. She didn't know what was behind it, but she knew it was dangerous. A revelation that couldn't be undone or undiscovered. Whatever it was, it was affecting her work. She couldn't let it.

After another night of sleep, her back had recovered from the stakeout. She was tempted to stay home again, regardless. Kasia stared at the wall, watching the light move across her brother's drawings. Then she remembered the day. Delivery day for the Lavender.

It was enough to get her up and dressed. The quicker she learned Sophia's secret, the less leverage Sam would have to send her on more terrible jobs. She found bread, fresh from her mother's bakery run, in the kitchen and slathered it with jam. Kasia ate it while turning over the plan for Sophia she'd started in the warehouse. She'd have to overcome the less than gentlemanly first impression she'd made. She'd also have to figure out how not to fall apart in front of the woman again if she hinted at Kasia's own secrets. But the possibility of getting what she needed lit a fire in her she'd been afraid was extinguished yesterday.

It meant she'd have to spend more time with Sophia. She'd have to find her friends, get them talking about her. Watch her flit around the Lavender and any other usual haunts. She was determined to learn the woman inside and out, pick her pieces apart until she figured out what she knew about Harding.

Which meant Sophia would learn her, too. Almost inevitably. At least a little. She already knew too much, on instinct alone, if their last interaction was anything to go by. The thought made her queasy. It also woke her up, pounded on her chest. It wasn't like the feeling she usually got when she was onto something good. But it was close enough. She didn't want to contemplate what was different about it.

Kasia finished her breakfast and left for the warehouse, checking her watch on the way out. Only a few short hours until she'd see Sophia. Almost immediately, she corrected herself: only a few hours until she put her new plan in motion.

\* \* \*

Outside the door to the Lavender, Kasia had to pause to collect her thoughts. Now that she was here, the assurance she'd felt that morning was shaky. The prospect of seeing Sophia after their encounter last week made her throat close up. Her words echoed in Kasia's head: *You might enjoy spending time with people who don't judge what you are... or what you like.* Was Sophia trying to rattle her, shift the balance of power into her own hands? Or did she really see straight through her, shine a floodlight on the secrets she guarded in the dark? Kasia wasn't sure which possibility made her more anxious. Either way, she was going to have to make nice with Sophia if she wanted to put her new plan in motion. That is, if she didn't drop dead from nerves before she even made it across the Lavender's threshold.

Getting a good opportunity between her teeth sharpened her edges. She knew she was onto something when she dropped from her head, where she was usually locked in with thoughts circling like sharks, and into her body. She'd suddenly feel her fingers, electric and hot, and the firm press of the ground against her feet. It was a sensation of perfect balance, head blissfully clear, gut leading the charge. This was different. Kasia felt her hands, her feet, the burning stone in her stomach. But it didn't come with the clarity she was used to. Her brain felt like a crowded room, her thoughts an overlapping chatter.

She had Stan and Henry wait in the truck. Kasia didn't know how she'd respond when she saw Sophia, and she didn't want them to witness their conversation. Kasia found Sophia behind the bar. She was dressed casually in a pleated skirt and a blouse with a wide collar. She might be a secretary or a shopkeeper. Her elegance, however, still drifted off her like the scent of perfume. She was writing something, tallying numbers. Sophia seemed to glow. Or rather, it was like the darkness of the basement couldn't touch her, fleeing from her edges. Kasia couldn't feel her feet anymore; the sight of Sophia drew her forward.

Sophia, however, didn't even bother to look up at Kasia as she approached. Not a strong start to her plan. Kasia leaned against the bar on her elbow and set her hat down before smoothing back her hair. She offered a smile, cocking her eyebrow. "It's nice to see you, Ms. Worley."

"Mmm." Sophia's pen moved up and down the columns of numbers, hovering just above the paper. "I think I owe you an apology, Mr. Kasowski."

"An apology?" Kasia thought again about how she'd leaped into Sophia's car. "Why?"

Sophia paused and looked up at Kasia's face. Her eyes looked enormous underneath her lashes. The rim of dark paint around them made her green irises glow. "I... startled you, I think, and that was unkind." She worried the inside of her cheek, the skin dimpling between her teeth.

Kasia felt suspended in the air, unsure of how to move. She thought again of Sophia's gaze roaming her body, the insinuation in her voice when they'd last parted. She wasn't sure she'd call the feeling it gave her *startled*. Terrified, maybe. Naked. "Shocked" would be generous.

There had been another feeling, though. Far more shameful. A glimmer of hope; the tiny, lustrous joy of being seen. Remembering it called it back. A revived ember burning with the memory of the fire that created it.

None of what she'd felt then—what she felt again now—was anything she wanted to say out loud, even if she knew how. The quiet between them was stretching uncomfortably. Kasia could only think to cover it with politeness. "I'm sure you didn't mean offense," she offered tentatively.

"Not offense, no." Sophia straightened her spine. The woman eyed her up and down, as she had the last night Kasia had visited the Lavender. This time, her gaze was thoughtful—eyes narrowed, lips pursed, head cocked. Kasia shifted uneasily. The feeling of being in Sophia's spotlight returned. She tried to subtly wipe the sweat dripping down the back of her neck. Sophia's mouth opened, then closed, whatever she'd started to say cut short. Instead, she offered her mysterious half-smile, looked back down at her paper, and started tallying again. "I have a favor to ask."

"You aren't subtle, are you?" Kasia said. Anger crashed through her confusion. It brought the clarity she'd wanted, but made her forget she was supposed to play nice. "You're a new customer and you've already been late on a payment. You're not in a position for favors."

"I placed a very large order for tonight. Three times my last shipment."

"And?"

"And I've only got enough cash on hand to pay you for twice as much." Sophia put her pen down and rose, finally meeting Kasia's eyes squarely. "I'll have the rest for you tonight by midnight."

Suspicion that Sophia was using her confused feelings against her rose along with bile in her throat. Kasia pushed herself back to standing, suddenly wary. "I'm not in the habit of providing liquor on credit, Ms. Worley. But you seem to be in the habit of expecting it already."

Sophia sighed. Kasia noticed that she'd pinned her hair

hastily. A longer curl had escaped and hung down the back of her neck. She hardly knew Sophia, but seeing her frazzled felt unnatural. "We're a brand-new club, catering to a niche clientele. We don't have endless stores of cash on hand. But we're good for it. We've got an event tonight that all but promises it." Her fingers found the stray curl and pinned it back again. Kasia had a sudden, embarrassing thought about what it would be like to see her pull each pin from her hair. She imagined the curls in a wild halo around Sophia's face. As if she could read Kasia's thoughts, Sophia's voice dropped into a purr. "You might like the show, too. Even the kids from the rich neighborhoods will be coming."

Kasia pushed back hard from the bar. She was almost certain Sophia was taking advantage of her now. She shoved her hat back on her head, not realizing it was askew. "Ms. Worley," she said, her voice lowering into a growl. "I'm here to enforce your contract, and your contract doesn't care about good nights or bad nights. Your *contract*," Kasia picked up the piece of paper with the orders Sophia had been tallying and waved it, "says that when we deliver it, you pay for it. If you can pay for two-thirds of your order, you get two-thirds of your order. You run out of liquor, that's not my problem."

Sophia stared back, but seemed lost in thought. Kasia could see a muscle in her jaw twitching rhythmically. "Fifteen percent on the late third. By midnight."

"The whole order. If it's not paid in full, it's late," Kasia argued.

"Twenty on the late third."

"Twenty-five."

Sophia winced. "Fine. Twenty-five."

"Twenty-five." Kasia held out her hand. "And it goes to thirty if you don't have the rest by midnight."

"Deal." Sophia shook her hand, her grip firmer than Kasia expected. When Kasia turned around, Stan and Henry had wandered in and were watching her with confusion. She pointed up the stairs. "Well? Go get the rest. We've got more papers to deliver." The two men scurried towards the exit.

Sophia watched them go. "Neat trick," she said to Kasia. "Do they roll over, too?"

Kasia shot Sophia a glare. "Midnight," she repeated.

"Midnight." Sophia jerked her head towards the door. "Now go on. I've got work to do. And you've got papers to deliver."

# Chapter Fifteen

**M**aking nice might not have gone as well as Kasia hoped, but at least she'd scored an opportunity to return to the Lavender. Sophia wasn't pulling her leg about the turnout that night. At eleven, it was packed shoulder to shoulder with a joyfully gender-bending crowd. Black and white, chattering in German, Russian, Polish, Greek, and even Arabic. Wealthy slummers and neighborhood locals. Everyone was dolled up, the room a roiling wave of color. Sequins flashed, feathers swayed, fringe swung. The sharp tuxes on some of the men were only exceeded in tailoring by the tuxes on an equal number of women, bright pocket squares matched perfectly with their ties. A woman on stage performed a vaudeville comedy routine—or wait, she realized, a man in elaborate stage makeup, with a dress that rivaled a film star's. She bantered with a young couple standing in front of the audience, sending the crowd into uproarious laughter.

Kasia stuck to the edge of the room, weaving her way towards the bar. Sophia was nowhere to be seen. Of course, Sophia was short, and harder to spot at a distance with so many people around. "Excuse me," she said to a group of three around a small table. "Can I borrow a chair?"

"We're using these," said an indignant man.

"Oh, only for a moment. I'm not sitting down." Kasia shooed him and he stood, despite looking affronted. She stepped onto the chair, balancing carefully as she scanned the heads below.

The drag queen on stage locked eyes with Kasia. "Oh doll, if you wanted my attention, you got it," she called. "Bring him up here."

Realizing her mistake, Kasia jumped down, hoping to disappear into the crush of people and avoid her fate. But the excited crowd pushed her forward until she was at the foot of the stage, then standing on it. The woman pulled her towards the microphone. "What's your name, honey?"

Kasia cleared her throat. "Andrew. Kasowski." The way her voice echoed through the mic made her wince.

"Oh, are you Polish?" she asked. Kasia nodded. "I love a Polish man. Such big families. Such big... appetites," she said, her hand gesturing over Kasia's lower half. "Must be all those meat and potatoes they eat. I'm a big fan of meat and potatoes myself." She threw the crowd an exaggerated wink, and they met her with peals of laughter. "They don't make me look like that, though." Kasia was scooting towards the edge of the stage. "Aw, he's shy. I won't torture you any more, honey. You might still be the center of MY attention once I'm off this stage, though. Everyone give Andrew a hand." The crowd cheered. Kasia gave a sheepish wave and hurried down the steps on the side of the platform.

The steps spit her out right next to the backstage door. It was propped open to let air circulate the small room. A handful of performers were tweaking makeup and pinning costumes. For a moment, Kasia was lost in the sight. She'd always been fascinated watching women put on makeup, even if she'd never wanted to herself. The skillful transformation felt like watching magic bloom from their fingers. This was a whole room—however small—of people transformed. The club had plenty of gender-benders, people she'd watched with equal parts interest and trepidation. But she was suddenly aware of the exaggeration in the performer's costumes, the joy, the fearlessness. It made her breath freeze in her chest. She felt elated, and at the same time a sick envy. A hovering, lonely stranger outside the warmly-lit home of a raucous family.

The feeling sunk deeper when she realized Sophia was in the middle of the room, and she was hanging off of Maude Hogan's arm. Her head was thrown back in a free, easy laugh Kasia hadn't even thought her capable of.

Maude Hogan was a legend. Not just in Detroit, but all over the country. She sang bawdy, vaudevillian blues, and Kasia was fairly certain even the most proper people knew how to belt her songs once you got a few drinks in them. Maude often performed in male drag, as she apparently was tonight—her tall, broad, curvaceous form both intimidating and undeniably charismatic. Her dark brown skin shone luminously in the backstage lights, set off by the white contrast of her perfectly fitted tuxedo shirt.

Kasia tried to recover her confidence as she approached them. It sounded like the two were remembering a wild night in Chicago— how long ago, Kasia wondered? It annoyed her that Maude noticed her first. Kasia was tall, but Maude was taller; and as Maude turned to open the conversation to Kasia, Kasia hated that she had to lift her head up to meet the woman's eyes. Bawdy act or not, Maude had toured all over the world. She had undeniable talent. And she looked damned handsome in a suit. Kasia felt completely outclassed, like a scrawny kid standing next to her. She hoped a cocky grin could cover it. "Maude Hogan. Never thought I'd have the pleasure of meeting you." She held out a hand. "Andrew Kasowski."

Maude returned the grin and a firm handshake. "Pleasure to meet you, Andrew." Maude looked at Sophia and gestured towards Kasia with her chin. "This a friend of yours?"

Before Kasia could open her mouth, Sophia responded, "A business associate. One of our suppliers." Kasia hated how the laughter had fallen from her face, her half-smile in its place instead. "He's here to collect a debt from me."

"Well, if you're a fan, I hope you're staying for my act," said Maude. "I believe I'm up next."

"Wouldn't miss it," Kasia replied. As if on cue, there was a burst of applause from the audience, and the drag queen on stage trotted down the steps to the backstage room. She exchanged cheek kisses with Maude, then threw a wink at Kasia that made her blush.

"Ah, my bashful boy. We meet again," the queen said. "Friend of Sophia's?"

"Liquor supplier," Kasia said, trying to keep the bitterness from her tone. The queen didn't respond, already pushing her way between two performers to check her makeup in a mirror.

"Break a leg," Sophia called after Maude as she headed towards the stage. Sophia trailed behind her, followed by Kasia, until they could see enough of the stage to watch Maude settle in next to the microphone.

She welcomed the crowd, letting the frantic cheers die down before gesturing to the band to start. Her rich voice would have filled the room even without a mic. The song was a crowd favorite, a blues number that barely hid the fact that it was about a woman with female lovers. Kasia had heard it mimicked by other singers in other clubs. Hearing it now, though, in a crowd that could appreciate and understand it in a way the other venue's patrons couldn't, sent an odd shiver through her. It was as though the song weaved a spell, connecting every soul in the packed room. Most of them, at least—the slummers there for a scandalous performance, rather than comradery, merely looked titillated. Still, the spectacle of it didn't dampen the excitement and courage the song, and Maude's undeniable stage presence, seemed to lend the queer listeners.

Despite watching the performance with rapt attention, Sophia spared Kasia a glance. It quickly twisted into a longer, more thoughtful look. She smiled—not the half-smile she usually offered, but a full one, and strangely tentative. "Are you enjoying the performance?" she asked, barely audible above the band.

"She's brilliant," Kasia answered honestly. While jealousy still tightened her chest, Kasia knew she couldn't hide the starry look in her eyes. The music, and the feeling it gave her, was too overwhelming.

"Have you seen her perform before?" Sophia said.

Kasia shook her head. "No. I know the song, but I've never seen her play it." Kasia scooted closer, leaning in close to her ear so that she could be heard above the music. "So, how do you know Maude Hogan?" She tried to sound casual, but it came out sharper than intended.

The other woman examined Kasia for a moment, a curious look passing over her face. Her cheek twitched, like she was suppressing a broader smile. "We've known each other for years. We've frequented the same clubs, we're acquainted with the same people. We were intimate friends for a time."

Kasia swallowed to calm her flipping stomach, hands clenched into fists in her pockets. "Were?"

Was it Kasia's imagination, or did Sophia's smile spread a little wider? If so, it disappeared as quickly as it came. Sophia turned her head back towards the stage. "She's so famous now, she's always on the road. Hard to keep in touch. She's at the Lavender as a favor. She's due to perform back-to-back shows for the Graystone, and came early just for us tonight." The thought washed her face with relief. "Hard to get a club started, much less keep it going. With her bringing a crowd this early, we might have a chance."

"You must have been pretty good friends for her to do all that for you," Kasia said. She pinned her eyes on the stage now as well. The way Maude's presence filled the space was captivating. Kasia could've sunk into her performance without coming up for air if her attention wasn't locked on Sophia.

"Girls like us have to look out for each other when we can." The two women couldn't have been more different, but Sophia didn't have to explain what she meant. The place they stood said enough. "No one else will." Her eyes shifted to the floor. "And sometimes you've got no choice but to look after yourself." She looked back at the stage.

"I understand," Kasia said. Her own world was full of favors, trades, negotiation, survival, secrets. She wondered how much of Sophia's was as well. And for the first time she realized that the openness here, in this basement gin-joint, was sacred and tenuous. Speakeasies always operated on borrowed time. They were only as permanent as the next police raid. But they weren't always sanctuaries.

It filled her with a panic she struggled to identify. She could only wonder if the relationships between the women here were, by necessity, just as temporary. If every love meant knowing loss. She suddenly wanted to leave. She could barely look at Sophia.

Which was difficult, because Sophia had turned to face her after Kasia's response. "Do you?" Sophia said. Kasia could barely hear her over the music. Despite the assurance in Sophia's words, her expression was questioning, almost hesitant. Her eyes swept Kasia's figure again.

"In my way." The press of the crowd kept them close. Only inches of bare space separated them. If Kasia leaned forward, just a little, she was sure she could feel the heat radiating from Sophia's skin. Sophia's face was tilted up, just beneath Kasia's. She pictured dipping her head, pressing her lips to Sophia's. She could almost taste her mouth, feel the slip of her tongue, Sophia's breath on her cheek.... Cheeks that were flushed, burning hot. Was it her imagination, or were Sophia's as well? The woman looked less uncertain now. Instead, she had an almost hungry look, her eyes tracing Kasia's, then falling just slightly to her lips.

The song ended, and the swell of applause tore Kasia's attention away. What was she doing? She was losing her head. Getting friendly with Sophia was one thing. Whatever was passing between them was another. It was too close, too intimate. Too much like revealing her secret. Kasia stepped back, though she hardly had room to put more space between them. "It's nearly midnight," she said, stiff.

Sophia's face collapsed into a scowl. She tossed her head, arms crossed over her chest. "Can't it wait until after the performance?" The annoyance returning to Sophia's voice was a relief.

"Sure. I could use another 5% of your money," Kasia said. Her own voice was cold now. "We had a deal."

"Fine." She grabbed Kasia's hand, pulling her through the crowd towards the bar. The noise of the room, the voices, the music, glasses clinking and breaking, quieted to a soft hum that filled Kasia with a ripple of vibration. The angle of Sophia's arm let her glimpse the smooth skin at the top of her ribs. That inch of skin was all she could see. The room blurred and narrowed, her own heavy breath now beating in her ears.

And then Sophia let her hand go. The world around them returned, harsh and loud. Sophia ducked behind the bar, disappearing behind James. When she rose again, she was counting bills, which she held out to Kasia. "There. The remainder of my balance, at..." She pulled Kasia's wrist toward her, and pushed her jacket sleeve back to glance at her watch. "...11:58." Sophia tossed her head towards the stairs. "You got what you came for. Unless you're here to drink, make room for paying customers."

Maybe she wanted to imagine it, but Kasia thought Sophia sounded wounded. It didn't seem possible. Her instinct told her to test it in the only way she knew how. "No more liquor on credit," Kasia said, folding the bills and tucking them away in her wallet. "Not unless you want to pay premium. You're proving yourself to be a risky customer, Ms. Worley."

"I didn't think you were so scared of risk, Mr. Kasowski. It's rather a disappointment to know you don't have the stomach for it." It was amazing how expressive that half-smile could be. It had turned cruel, as pointed as her lipstick cupid's bow drawn on sharply in red. "Nothing is less appealing in a man than cowardice."

She was good at getting a last word in. Maybe it was the advantage of her short stature, but in a quick moment, she'd disappeared completely between onlookers.

Kasia knew that she'd pushed Sophia, but she couldn't help but feel stung by her dismissal. As eager as she'd been to leave moments ago, she was reluctant now—and not just because of Sophia. The Lavender was a fantasy, a fairytale. Maybe, she thought, an Otherworld where she could have been, if only she'd known how to cross its threshold when she was younger and could make different choices.

But it made her think of all the fairytales she knew. She thought of the stories of the men-wolves her mother told her and her brother; of the demon's dance, of Jonek. Fairytales often ended in tragedy, especially when the characters in stories were greedy for things they couldn't—shouldn't —have.

Her mother's house was hers. The back of the paper supply with the liquor bottles hidden in reams of newsprint. The gun hidden in her jacket and the knife in her boot. Delivery routes that Sam had entrusted to her. The cash she hid. The respect of her boys. They were more than she'd ever hoped to have. They already invited an unhappy ending.

But just like the characters in the fairytales, she wanted to reach for more.

# Chapter Sixteen

It was unseasonably warm for early March. The back of the paper supply was stuffy. Kasia unbuttoned her shirt a few inches down her chest, her collar resting beside her on the table, and rolled her sleeves up to just below her elbows. She knew the dust in the air would settle into the light sheen of sweat on her skin, but she was too hot and irritated to care.

Sophia hadn't been at the Lavender when she accompanied the liquor drop earlier that afternoon. Her pride hadn't allowed her to ask James where Sophia was, and Kasia had to wonder if the woman was avoiding her. The other night, Sophia *had* to have felt... whatever it was Kasia felt. A gravitational pull, tense and terrifying. Fear still sat in Kasia's stomach like molten iron. It warred with another familiar feeling, one Kasia liked even less, even as she indulged it. She ached to touch Sophia. The smoothness of Sophia's skin, the give of her flesh, the warmth of her mouth—Kasia could almost feel it. She'd never touched or been touched so intimately. Since Andrew left, she was lucky for a familial embrace. Kasia thought it didn't bother her. But suddenly, it was the only thing on her mind. What would Sophia feel like? What would it be like to be held, caressed, kissed? What would it be like to make her throw her head back in laughter—like Maude did, Kasia thought sourly—or for her fingers to clasp around Sophia's?

Kasia stared down into the column of numbers in front of her and realized she'd been tapping her pen against the page, spreading a splotch of ink onto her careful calculations. Kasia scoffed, throwing the pen down to pinch the bridge of her nose. Her fingers smeared ink into the space between her eyes.

Stevie burst in through the door, pulling Kasia from her thoughts. Stevie clenched a newspaper in his meaty fist, waving it over his head like he was using it to hail a cab. "Andy!" His voice echoed against the brick walls, piercing into Kasia's skull like an icepick. "Andy, you see this?"

He threw the paper down in front of Kasia. She smoothed the wrinkled pages out to read the front-page headline: PURPLES, POLICE CLASH IN PUBLIC SHOOT-OUT; TWO OFFICERS AND BYSTANDER DEAD. Kasia glanced from the paper to Stevie. "Last night? How am I just now hearing about this?" The iron in her stomach churned. Violence was often a necessary part of the job, but a high-profile show of force brought unwelcome attention. It demanded blood in return. Whether it was her blood, or her boys', or the Purples themselves was out of her hands. She didn't like things out of her control.

Stevie stared at Kasia, mouth hanging open. "Sam hasn't called? Sent a message? Nothing?"

Kasia shook her head, scanning the article. *Police Chief Richard Harding condemned the violent act, stating, "Two brave men lost their lives to protect our city from street thugs and bootleggers. Their sacrifice, and the life of an innocent woman, will not be in vain. I will not rest until I've rooted out this nest of rats and exterminated every one of them."*

"The Purples have to be lying low after this. Who knows when Sam will reach out?" Kasia let out a heavy sigh. "Call the boys in for a meeting. I need everyone acting smart. Subtle drop-offs, no talking business in front of strangers. Act as if every move is being watched, because it might very well be." Kasia grabbed his arm. "Don't relay any of this on the phone. Just call them in. Got it?"

Stevie nodded. If he was offended that Kasia thought he might be sloppy enough to discuss business on a phone line, where someone could be listening in, he was gracious enough—or smart enough—not to show it. "When do you want them in?"

"Right now. As fast as they can get here."

"Right." Stevie hesitated for a moment, his eyes fixed on her forehead. "Boss, you got, uh... you got something, right there." He pointed between his own brows.

Kasia touched her head, then looked down at her ink-stained fingers. She closed her eyes for a moment, trying to push down the anger building inside her. "Thanks." She stood and headed towards the washroom. Her reflection showed a black mark, smeared between her eyes to her hair-line. Kasia heaved a sigh. There was nothing like a leaky pen to remind her she was losing control, not just over work, but her entire life.

# Chapter Seventeen

March 14th. 4:29. Kasia stood on Sophia's porch, watching the second hand on her watch creep closer to the half-hour. After the last meeting at the Lavender, and Sophia avoiding her since, Kasia wasn't sure if she'd be allowed in. She almost hadn't shown up. Only the urgency that the shootout brought made her keep her appointment. She had to keep her plan in motion. Get close to Sophia, find out what she had on the chief, give that information to Sam, and he'd keep Harding at bay. Despite the cold, she was sweating. The prospect of seeing Sophia again, no matter how remote, made her tremble. *Ten... nine....* She raised her fist, and only at the precise moment the clock hit 4:30, she knocked.

The door swung open. Behind it was the same pretty older maid from her first visit, who answered with the same stiff, polite smile. "Good afternoon, Mr. Kasowski. Do come inside."

"Thank you." Kasia stepped by her, eyes scanning the foyer. Dark woods, plush chairs, oil portraits and paintings of horses on the walls. A little out of fashion, like it was decorated at the turn of the century, but tasteful. The maid gestured to the first door off the hallway, a sitting room with a large hearth and distinctly Victorian furniture. Kasia followed her direction and settled onto a chaise lounge, the back carved into the form of a reclining swan. The maid disappeared, leaving Kasia alone in the grand little room. Her foot tapped as frantically as her heartbeat, the sound muffled by the thick rug beneath her.

And then Sophia appeared at the room's double doors. She wore a dress, or perhaps a robe—it had been so long since Kasia had worn women's clothing, she couldn't tell. It was a deep emerald green velvet that gathered at the waist with a gold clasp; the neck plunging to reveal something in cream silk and lace worn beneath it. It allowed Kasia a glimpse of her collarbones and the luminous skin of her chest beneath it. The sleeves were long and bell-shaped, trimmed with lace in the same color as the silk under layer. Her face was made-up, although more lightly than Kasia had seen before; the eyes ringed only in dark lashes, while her signature dark lipstick colored her lips. For once, Kasia was wordless, the breath knocked out of her like she'd taken a fist to the gut. She shot to standing. Sophia smiled—a full smile, not the half-smile Kasia could picture with the detail of a film reel. She seemed to know the effect she was having on Kasia and liked it. "You kept your appointment," Sophia said.

Kasia's throat was dry. It took her a few moments to collect herself enough to answer. "Yes," she said finally. Kasia took off her hat and held it in front of her. "I think we got off on the wrong foot." She squirmed, shifting from side to side. "I think it's my turn to apologize for, uh... startling you."

"When did you startle me?" Sophia moved to perch on

the edge of a couch across from her, the dress skimming her hips and thighs as she walked.

Kasia could feel her face burning and hated it. "Not startled, I suppose." Sophia's apology had lingered so long in her mind, she thought surely the woman would understand. Apparently, she'd dwelled on it far less often than Kasia. "But I think I offended you the last time we spoke."

"Oh, that?" Sophia gestured for her to sit, and Kasia obeyed. "No, not offended. Confused, perhaps." Sophia picked up a bell from the table between them and rang it. "Magda?" The maid appeared at the door. "Could you please bring us some tea, and perhaps something a little stronger for our guest? Thank you." Magda nodded, and Sophia turned back to Kasia. "Just as I'm confused about why you kept your appointment. I assume you're not here about the Lavender's liquor order. We paid in full this week."

"No."

The other woman tilted her head. "Then why don't you tell me why you've dropped by?"

"I...." The word came out pinched and raspy. Kasia cleared her throat. "I suppose... I suppose I wanted to know more about you."

"Ah." Was that disappointment in Sophia's tone? "About how I know Harding, you mean?"

Kasia squirmed in her seat. "Do you mind if I take off my jacket? It's awfully warm in here."

"Please, make yourself comfortable." Magda entered again, pushing a bar cart carefully filled with a teapot, liquor bottles, and cups and glasses. "Thank you, Magda. You can close the door behind you." Kasia wasn't sure if she felt relief or trepidation as the doors swung shut.

She stripped off her jacket, throwing it beside her on the

chaise. She was sure it wasn't proper, but she didn't know what else to do with it. Sophia poured two cups of tea, then motioned to the liquor. "What would you like to drink?"

"Uh... a whiskey, please. Neat." Sophia nodded and pulled a bottle from the cart, pouring the amber liquid into a short glass. Kasia accepted it gratefully and drank it in a single swig, the burn contorting her face. Sophia poured her another two fingers before taking a sip of her tea. Discussing Harding seemed impossible, even as the liquor burned in her stomach.

Kasia tapped her finger against her glass. Sophia waited, her hands clasped around her crossed knee. She decided on the only other topic that came to mind. "I meant it," Kasia said finally, "that I want to know about you."

Sophia tilted her head. "Why?" It wasn't combative or suspicious, but genuine curiosity.

Kasia paused, searching for the words. She and words had never gotten along. She hoped the buzz and heat of the whiskey she'd downed would help. "I've never met a woman like you." Kasia cringed at the cliché and tried again. "What I mean is... I've never met a woman so...open about her...preferences."

Sophia took another sip of tea, taking her time with the answer. "My preferences?" A laugh twitched on her cheeks. She set the cup down on the table. "You mean I prefer the company of women?"

"You seem to," Kasia said.

Sophia shrugged and sipped her tea. "What about it interests you?"

Kasia wanted to crawl under the very expensive Persian rug under her feet. She came to get to know Sophia, and instead Sophia had talked her into a corner. Almost effort-lessly. Kasia was silent, unsure how to move.

Sophia smiled—a full smile again. Warmth spread through Kasia. She could feel her ears getting hot. "Who are you, Andrew?"

The question stopped the spreading warmth in its tracks. Kasia pinned her eyes on some European landscape rendered in oil behind Sophia's head. "What do you mean?" Her voice was stiff. "Andrew Kasowski. I run the Hamtramck Gang. What else do you need to know?"

Sophia's brows furrowed, her smile falling into a concentrated line. "There's something else. I saw your face during Maude's performance. You're hiding something. I want to know what it is."

Kasia stood abruptly and walked to the fireplace, heat be damned. She had to move. The spotlight on her was too bright, and the crackling embers gave her something to look at that wasn't Sophia's questioning face. "What did you see?" She was aiming for aggressive, a conversation-ender more than in inquiry. She was supposed to be probing Sophia, not the other way around. But it came out softer than she'd intended. She needed to know.

"Recognition," Sophia said. She switched her crossed legs and leaned against the back of the sofa, propping her head in her hand. "And longing."

Kasia stared hard into the fireplace, her heart pounding. She thought her silence was answer enough, but Sophia continued. "You said you want to know more about me. Tell me your truth, and I'll tell you mine."

Kasia ran a hand over the back of her neck. She couldn't stop twitching. She'd been in plenty of hairy situations, but none that made her feel so cornered.

She should have known better than to try to cozy up to a veteran woman-lover. If anyone could sniff out her secrets— all of them—it would be Sophia. Kasia retrieved her jacket from the chaise and pulled out her cigarettes, lighting one shakily. She hated herself for being here, in Sophia's fancy house, in the exact position of inevitable confession she'd fought for years.

Because she *did* want to tell Sophia. That small, secret voice in her, not so small now after all, was screaming for it. It wanted someone to know. More than that, it wanted *her* to know.

Kasia thudded back down into her seat, rubbing her forehead. Sophia's promise—truth for truth—suddenly eclipsed her concerns. Sophia knowing her truth made Kasia more vulnerable than she'd ever been. But maybe it was worth it to get Sophia to open up. She didn't expect Sophia to confess everything she had on Harding, but Kasia might get closer to figuring it out.

"Kasia," she said. She leaned against her knees, hands and head dangling. "I was born Kasia Kasowski. Andrew is my brother." She glanced up at Sophia, who was taking in this information with surprisingly little response. What had Kasia expected—triumph? Smugness? Shock? None of them registered on the other woman's face. Kasia continued. "Was my brother, I guess. He disappeared in the war."

Sophia nodded. "Ah, I see." She thought for a moment. "Do you prefer being Andrew? Are you more yourself?"

Kasia hesitated before the words came out in a rush. "In some ways. I never liked dresses, or any of the things I was told I had to do as a girl. And I like the ways I can move in the world, ways I never could before. But... it feels strange, living as my brother. He was different from me. I'm more myself living as him, but I'm still not fully me."

Sophia nodded. Her smile was back, and gentle. "Do you prefer I call you Andrew? Or something else?"

Kasia's mind stopped for a moment, feeling like a glass

shot through with a bullet. It had never occurred to her that she could live as she did and still be called by her own name by anyone. "Kasia," she said finally. "You can call me Kasia."

"A beautiful name," Sophia said. "It's nice to meet you, Kasia." Her voice was softer than Kasia had ever heard it. It wrapped her in comfort. She fought the urge to throw her arms around Sophia, tears prickling her eyes. She felt raw all over, and at the same time, so light. She'd never felt this weightless.

Kasia rubbed her eyes, hoping it didn't make them redder. Sophia took another sip of tea, taking her time before her next question. "How long have you been living as Andrew?"

"Ten years or so," Kasia answered. She tried to keep her voice even.

"And how did you come about it?"

"Well... my mother got sick. She couldn't work much. I had to find something to keep us both afloat." Sophia nodded, her attention rapt, expression open and soothing. Something about it felt more compelling than a priest in a confessional. "After my brother went missing during the war, I did what I had to."

"That's noble of you," Sophia said. Kasia wondered for a moment if it was sarcasm, but if so, Sophia didn't betray it.

"You said you'd tell me about you if I told you about me," Kasia ventured. She'd fought to piece herself back together, but her hands were still shaking. She took a drag from her cigarette, hoping to calm her nerves.

"What do you want to know?" Sophia asked.

"You... aren't married?" Kasia said.

"I was married. For three years, in Chicago."

"Oh?"

"Nicholas died in the war as well." Sophia laid back a little, as if waiting for a response she knew was coming.

"I'm sorry. For you and his family," Kasia said. She'd known enough grief for the response to feel limp. But anything people said in the wake of a death was lackluster. There were no words for what it did to you.

Sophia tilted her head. "Thank you," she said. She must have responded to Kasia's sentiment a hundred times, but she sounded as though she meant it. "When he enlisted, I followed him to Europe. I landed in London and trained as a nurse at the Endell Street Military Hospital."

"You did?" Kasia's eyes widened. She'd heard of Endell Street before. It was famous for being staffed entirely by suffragettes, right down to the surgeons.

"I did. You could say I found myself there." Sophia's mysterious half-smile was back. "I realized I wanted to live on my own terms, to work for myself. Not in medicine—I had my fill of that. I wanted to, well... create a space, for people like me." For a moment, she looked wistful. "London was the first time I met other women who preferred women. I fell in love for the first time there. Regina was her name. Another nurse. But her parents were eager for her to marry, and I had my husband."

Sophia paused. "Losing him was very difficult. He was a good man. Or boy, really. We were so young. But he loved me, and I regret that I couldn't love him. Not in the way he wanted."

Kasia bit and released her lip. "What happened to Regina?"

"Once the war ended, her parents pushed hard for her to marry. Regina didn't want to disappoint them." She shrugged, although her eyes looked dark. "It's hard to live as we do. Families often turn their backs if they know. It's why

I didn't want to depend on anyone, not my parents, not a husband. I realized, in London, that I'd do anything to live just as I pleased."

A long silence passed between them. "And how did you manage that?"

Sophia pulled into herself a little. Just enough for Kasia to notice. "Nicholas had family money." Her voice was suddenly cool. "Enough for me to establish myself here."

The shift in her tone threw Kasia, but she tried not to show it. "You're a remarkable woman," Kasia said. Her eyes locked on her feet.

Sophia examined Kasia closely. Kasia could feel her gaze on her, sweeping over her body. "So are you," Sophia said. She heard the whispering movement of the velvet robe. And then Sophia was next to her on the chaise. Closer than Kasia had ever been to her, their thighs pressed together. Sophia smelled of dark, toasted spices in wine. Her hand slid over Kasia's, and her touch was everything Kasia had imagined it to be. Soft, warm, and electrifying.

"I hope you feel we've had a better start now?" Sophia's voice was barely a murmur, so close to Kasia's ear that she could feel her breath caress her cheek. Sophia cupped Kasia's chin in her palm and turned her face towards her own. Kasia felt pinned in Sophia's gaze, blank, breathless, the world spinning on the axis of Sophia's skin on hers.

It was almost painful, that lightest of touches. Sophia's lingering fingers filled Kasia with so much need, so much desire, and at the same time, so much fear that it felt like holding her hand to a fire for warmth and coming too close to the flame. Kasia leaped to her feet. "Yes, thank you," she said. It tumbled out of her, rapid and breathless. "I'll see you next week?"

Sophia's eyes widened as her face fell. "Of course."

Kasia tore out of the room without saying goodbye. She was already at the front door when she heard Sophia call out, "Wait" from behind her. With every bit of courage she had, she turned to face the other woman. Sophia was breathless, her chest moving rapidly up and down beneath the velvet and silk. "Come by the Lavender sometime," she said. "Not for work. Just to see what it's like. I'll introduce you around." A lock of hair had escaped its pin in her rush to catch Kasia. Kasia watched, fingers itching with jealousy, as she tucked it behind her ear. "You might like it."

Kasia nodded. She mumbled quick thanks before disappearing into the late afternoon. She moved so quickly that by the time she looked back up, she was three unfamiliar streets away from Sophia's home. Kasia paused, taking in deep, gulping breaths like she'd emerged from water near-drowning. It would be dark soon and her jacket was inside-out.

Kasia cursed, leaning over to clutch her knees, chest heaving. Humiliated tears stung her eyes. Why had she run? Why was something she wanted desperately so terrifying?

The answer came quickly: before today, Kasia told herself that Sophia might still think she was a man. An embarrassing man, against whom Sophia could weaponize her charms for favors despite her clear preferences, who'd turn his tail and run if she implied he might like the company of other men. But a man all the same.

But Sophia's preferences *were* clear; she'd stated them boldly. Just before she'd sat next to Kasia. When she'd gotten so close, Kasia would only have had to raise her head for their lips to meet. And there had been no deal, no favor on the table.

The only explanation was that she'd been right the first

time Sophia hinted at her inversion. Sophia had seen straight through the suit, the carefully crafted persona she pieced together from herself and her twin. She'd plucked out Kasia's two biggest secrets and laid them between them. Hell, she'd gotten Kasia to confess one herself.

It felt like touching a tender wound. No matter how gentle Sophia had been, the pain was too much to bear. Wanting it didn't matter. The pain pulled her back.

Kasia was so busy brooding over what she'd wanted that it didn't dawn on her until the next day that she hadn't gotten what she'd needed, either. If anything, Sophia's relationship with Chief Harding was more confusing than ever. If she was so clear in her preferences, it didn't seem like she was hiding an affair with him. Then what did she know that had him running to answer her call?

# Chapter Eighteen

Watching couples stream into the Fox Theatre was grating on Kasia's nerves. Every arm wrapped around arm seemed to settle under her skin, itching. Every woman's ample laugh mocked her cowardice. She'd never backed down from a challenge, much less passed up an opportunity to pluck exactly what she wanted from a situation. Sophia, though... she made Kasia run on a different kind of instinct. She felt like a hunter that turned tail and ran once they'd cornered their prey. It was maddening.

She needed the jump on Harding. Anything, at this point. If Sam was impatient before, it would only be worse after the shootout. Whether or not she knew it, Sophia was in greater danger by the day. And Kasia's attempts to figure Harding out without harming Sophia were landing her flat on her face, humiliation after humiliation. If she couldn't get Sophia to share what she had on Harding yet, she'd have to find other resources. Something that would hold Sam off for a while.

She'd sucked down three cigarettes by the time Officer

Ward showed up. Kasia was too busy staring at her feet to see him approach. He hissed into her ear as he clutched her arm, "We have to meet someplace more private."

Kasia jumped. She shoved Officer Ward away. "What the hell is wrong with you? Don't sneak up on a man like that."

Officer Ward reeled back, nearly falling over. Once he righted himself, he tugged at his coat, indignant. "Watch it, Andrew. Don't make me take you in for assaulting an officer."

Kasia pinched the bridge of her nose. This was not improving her day. "Privacy. Fine. Walk with me."

Officer Ward fell into step behind her, hands shoved in his pockets. "What did you do to get on the Chief Harding's watch list?" he said as they left the crowd behind. "He's been sniffing around, asking questions about you. I can't have anyone knowing I'm involved with any of the shit you've got going on, you hear me?"

Kasia motioned towards an alley. They took a few steps into the dark. "He connected me with Sam."

"No shit, he connected you with Sam. You probably handle a quarter of liquor delivered for this city."

Kasia snorted. "I wish it was a quarter." She took a roll of cash out of her coat and held it out. "You're not backing out of our deal, are you?"

The officer heaved a sigh. He leaned back against the wall, arms crossed. "I've got kids to feed. I can't put my ass on the line for you."

Kasia bristled. "Kids to feed, sure. Six of them, right? Four with your wife, two with your mistress. That's a lot of mouths. And shoes. And school supplies. You've got another on the way, don't you? With the mistress, I mean."

Officer Ward gaped. "How do you...."

"It doesn't matter how. I know what I know. And I know you need money for expenses. Better money than the city pays. You know what else is expensive? Divorce. Your mistress would be happy, at least."

The man squinted his eyes shut, shaking his head towards the ground. "Fine." He looked up at Kasia. "This is the last time." The officer grabbed the still-outstretched money and shoved it into his pocket.

"It's only the last time if I say it is." Kasia leaned her arm against the wall behind him, looming. Instinct prickled, hot. She bit down on it and smiled. "I'll tell you what. I'll let you out of our deal, but I need something big."

"What?" Officer Ward shrunk away from her.

"I need you to find out which joints Harding is planning to raid." Kasia tapped his chest. "You bring me a list, and I'll let you off the hook."

"I can't do that," Officer Ward protested. "The chief doesn't give that information out to just anyone. I don't know where we're hitting until I get the order."

"Someone knows. Harding, a couple of confidants. There's a plan. The plan requires coordination, and that means somewhere, it's on a piece of paper. Find it, and it's the last thing I'll ask you to do for me." Kasia eased herself upright, rolling her shoulders. "And if you don't, I'll have to have a conversation with your wife. Do we have a deal?"

The officer slumped. "Fine. But I better never see you again once we're through."

Kasia shrugged. "Can't promise that. But if you get what I need, I'll try to keep my distance."

Officer Ward straightened his jacket and tugged his hat over his eyes. "I'll have it for you next week."

"You'll have it in three days," Kasia said. "By whatever means necessary."

He didn't try to argue. Kasia knew then that he'd come through.

# Chapter Nineteen

Her talk with Ward soothed Kasia's confidence. Unfortunately, it only magnified how much she wanted to see Sophia. It was like a twitch that wouldn't stop. She stared at the numbers in her ledger, unable to hold them long enough in her mind to add and subtract. She'd start, and then Sophia would invade her thoughts, always accompanied by a twist in her stomach and tightness in her throat that drove out the possibility of anything else.

"You okay?" Henry's voice, close and concerned, startled her. She hadn't heard him come into the warehouse's back room. "You look like hell."

Kasia glanced down at herself. Her trousers and shirt were disheveled. She could practically feel the dark circles carved under her eyes. And while she didn't know what her hair was doing, she'd been running her hands through it while trying to work, so it couldn't have been good. "Yeah." She leaned back and stretched. She could feel the bandages tight around her chest, pressing against the motion. "Trying to figure out how to get Harding off our backs."

Henry tilted his head. "Is that it?"

Kasia leveled her gaze at him. "That's not enough? It's my job to keep all of us as safe as I can, not to mention profitable. You worry about getting deliveries done, and I'll worry about everything else."

Henry looked wounded. "Look. I'm just saying, I've never seen you like this. Things come up, and you handle them."

"This isn't some stupid kids trying to sell bathtub gin in Sam's territory. It's not getting one do-gooder officer with a chip on his shoulder to back down. It's the Detroit Chief of Police, after Sam, me, and the rest of you." Kasia rubbed her eyes. "So no, I'm not my usual self." The words came out quietly. She wanted to hear the snap in her own voice, but exhaustion overrode it.

Henry crept around the desk. He hesitated before putting a gentle hand on her shoulder. He squeezed once, then withdrew, as if he thought she might turn on him and bite. "Hey. I get it. You've got a lot on your plate."

He didn't, couldn't, understand. But he was trying. Kasia could tell that much. She thought for a wild second about telling him everything. About Sophia, her confused feelings, and how difficult it made doing what she needed to do to get the information that could save them all.

She couldn't. It would be like rolling over on her back and showing her belly. Telling Sophia her real identity was one thing. While their worlds were connected by the liquor the Lavender required, they were separate enough. But that kind of honesty meant something different in her gang. She trusted Henry more than almost anyone else. He was a good egg. Reliable. But weakness was blood in the water. If not to Henry, then any man at the other end of his well-meaning loose lips. "Thanks," she said instead, and forced a smile.

He nodded and adjusted his hat. Kasia noticed that the feather on the brim perfectly matched the stripes on his shirt. Fucking Henry, the walking fashion plate. She'd never caught him disheveled. "I came by to see if you could do the deliveries with Stan tomorrow," he said. "My ma, she's got an appointment with the doctor. I'd like to be there. You know, just in case."

Kasia thought of her own mother, the countless doctor visits she'd accompanied her to. "Yeah, of course." Kasia squared her shoulders. "You should. Stan and I can handle it on our own."

Henry's shoulders relaxed from around his ears. "Thanks, boss." He turned to leave, then spun back slowly on his heel. "Maybe go out, take your mind off things for a while." He took a deep breath. "Go to one of the places we do deliveries for. You'll be treated like a king."

Kasia snorted. "Sure, until the next delivery comes and they start taking liberties because they think we're buddies."

"That Worley broad's place," Henry ventured. He took off his hat and fidgeted with the brim. "The pansy bar. You sorted out the problems there already, right? What could a drink hurt?"

Kasia froze at the mention of Sophia and the Lavender. She searched Henry's face. It was anxious, with an almost painful earnestness showing through. It broke Kasia into pieces to see. Henry had the sharpest mind of any guy she knew. He also had the biggest heart, too good for their line of work. He knew as well as she did that they couldn't speak openly about who Andrew really was, or what Kasia's preferences might be. It was the closest they'd ever come to Henry admitting he knew, and he loved her anyway.

For the second time in as many days, Kasia fought back tears. She wished she could embrace him. She wanted to thank him, to tell him what it meant. Instead, she inhaled sharply, straightened her back, and shrugged. "I suppose I did. I'll think on it, Henry."

He nodded, stuffed his hands in his coat pockets, and left. Kasia looked at her ledger and threw down her pen. For the first time since Andrew went missing, she let the tears come. She wasn't even sure why she was crying. It was all too much. The pressure to get Harding under control was one thing. She thrived off a good fight. It wasn't fighting that overwhelmed her. It was the surprising gentleness of Henry's support, of Sophia's softness in response to her confession. It was the way tenderness made her ache.

Tears landed on the ledger, smearing her columns of perfectly inked numbers. Kasia rubbed her wet face on her sleeve. For the first time, they looked meaningless, these stupid little records of her success. Books and books of numbers. She'd long since met most of the goals she'd set a decade ago. She'd kept her promise to Andrew, paid off her mother's house and made sure Gosia didn't need to work. She ran her own gang, and had the respect of her boys, her neighborhood, and Sam. She had stacks of cash that sat untouched and hidden. Kasia had never wanted the flash of money; she'd just wanted the security it brought. She had it now in spades. The only goal she hadn't achieved was becoming a Purple. It felt so close she could touch it—if only she could bring herself to get Sophia under her heel.

For the first time, Kasia couldn't remember why she'd wanted it in the first place.

She thought again of her mother's fairytales and the lives she could have lived. Would she have been happy living as openly as Sophia? It seemed, in many ways, like a life harder than her own. For one thing, she'd be fully dead in her mother's eyes, rather than playing a weird charade that kept Andrew alive and Kasia out of mind. She wondered how much Sophia's family knew, or if Sophia even cared what they thought.

And what was happiness worth anyway without security? How could she possibly move in the world as herself? Women were wearing pants now and then these days, but it wasn't just a matter of fashion. Everything about her screamed she was an invert, at least without the veneer of Andrew's identity. It always had, despite her family's attempts to turn her into a properly feminine woman. Who would employ a homosexual spinster?

But the Lavender's patrons were surviving somehow. They couldn't all come from money. Yet they were brave enough to seek others like themselves. They'd weighed the risks and decided that staying entirely hidden wasn't worth it. Kasia couldn't shake the feeling that they, like Sophia, knew something she didn't. Some part of the calculation that made their answer clear.

It terrified her. And she needed to know what it was.

# Chapter Twenty

Kasia spent an hour pacing in the kitchen before she left for the Lavender. Gosia eyed her wordlessly every time she passed through the room. Confusion, concern, annoyance—Kasia watched her mother's patience wear thin with each pass. Despite all of Kasia's tangled, complicated feelings vying for dominance, it was her desire to avoid her mother's displeasure that finally sent Kasia out into the cold.

The club was relatively quiet. Several tables were full, but no one played on the little stage. When Kasia found Sophia, sitting and laughing with a group clustered near the back of the room, her stomach lurched. She felt frozen and invisible at the bottom of the stairs, like she'd been suspended in ice while the world went on without her. She slunk to the bar, unsure if she wanted to be noticed or to maintain her inconspicuousness.

James, behind the bar, decided for her. "Mr. Kasowski. Sophia said we'd caught up with our payments."

"You did," Kasia said. "I'm just here for a drink."

She'd expected a raised eyebrow, maybe a pointed

comment. She'd have no response to either. Instead, James leaned against the counter and ran a hand through his salt-and-pepper hair. "Well, what'll you have?"

"I'll take an Old Fashioned." James nodded, already grabbing bottles from the shelves behind him. Moments later, she had a glass in front of her, and James was turning to a man who had taken the seat beside her.

"I'll take a highball," the man said. He was dressed in mechanic's overalls stained with machine grease and had a rough haircut that looked like it came from his mother's kitchen. But he had high cheekbones and kind-looking brown eyes, framed in soft creases. James set to work while Kasia sipped her drink. The play of rye and soda on her tongue was fortifying. From the corner of her eye, she watched the man beside her glance her over. "Haven't seen you before," he said. "You from out of town?"

Kasia set down her glass to look the man squarely in the face. "Born and raised in Hamtramck," she said.

"Polish?"

"Yes." She braced herself for his response. It wouldn't be the first time a stranger saw an excuse to unload their opinions about Poles.

"I speak a little," the man said instead. "I had a... dear friend, some years ago, who was Polish as well."

"Was?"

"He passed."

Kasia's eyes shifted back to her drink. She pulled the pack of cigarettes out of her pocket and set them in front of her before pulling one to her mouth. "I'm sorry. The war?"

"Tuberculosis. Can I bum one of those?"

Kasia pushed the pack down the bar towards the stranger. "Help yourself." He took a cigarette and held it out. His hands, despite being rough with hard labor, were surprisingly delicate. They looked like a bird in flight.

"Mind giving me a light?" Kasia flicked open her lighter and held it out. The man locked eyes with her as he leaned in, and Kasia suddenly understood that she was being sized up. He had full lips that pursed as he exhaled the smoke. Once he'd straightened, he held out a hand. "Michael."

She'd passed his assessment, but she had a feeling that she wasn't, in fact, what Michael was looking for. How to tell him that baffled her. She'd spent a decade protecting her secret. How did people like her communicate with one another without giving themselves away? She imagined a coded language, so foreign to her she didn't even know what it sounded like. It reminded her of reading. Shapes on paper that everyone around her knew made sounds, carried meaning, while she recognized only bits and pieces and made assumptions about the rest. "Andrew." She wasn't sure what else to say, so she offered a hand.

Michael took it and shook it firmly. "Is this your first time here, Andrew?"

"Not exactly." Kasia felt a struggle for words on her tongue. "I deliver for the club."

"I see. And curiosity got the better of you." Michael's brow raised, his expression mischievous.

"I'm here to see Sophia," she admitted.

Michael looked surprise. He swiveled on his stool to look towards Sophia's table. "Oh, honey. I think you might be barking up the wrong tree there."

Kasia felt her face flush. "Not exactly."

Michael's brows knit as he examined her more closely. Suddenly, his expression widened, jaw dropping with surprise. "Oh. Oh! I'm afraid it's me with the wrong tree." He burst into laughter. The sound drew Sophia's attention.

Her head rose, and she eyed the two of them. "I thought—well. You know what I thought. I'm terribly sorry." He patted Kasia's shoulder. "Welcome, all the same."

Sophia stood from the table. Her dress was green, with jet bead details, and in a gossamer material that seemed to slide over her hips as she walked. Kasia felt her heart rise to her throat. Sophia leaned against the bar at Kasia's side, so close that Kasia could feel the warmth radiating from her skin. "I see you've met our supplier."

Michael slid off his stool to kiss each of Sophia's cheeks. "Good to see you, sweetheart. How's tricks?"

"Oh, you know. We're still open, and that's something."

"It's very much something. Took you years to get here. Every moment counts." He gave her arm a companionable squeeze before looking back and forth between the two women. "Is that Rodger over there? I think I'll go say hello. Excuse me."

Kasia caught a quick wink that he threw to her over Sophia's shoulder. It was strangely comforting. Sophia swung herself onto Michael's abandoned stool, adjusting the fall of the fabric over her legs before turning to Kasia. "I didn't know if you'd actually come."

"I didn't know if I would either," Kasia admitted, every muscle tense. "I left your house... quickly, the other day. I felt like I should apologize." *Again,* she thought. She'd never apologized so much to anyone.

Sophia propped her chin on her hand. "I wasn't holding it against you," she said. "I didn't mean to make you uncomfortable."

"I wasn't," Kasia said. After a moment's hesitation, she added, "Maybe I was. But I don't think that was your fault."

Sophia tilted her head, sending a curled lock tumbling

over her eye. Kasia fought the urge to push it back. "Is that the only reason you came by?"

Kasia felt a knot form in her throat. "I wanted to see how business is going," she lied.

Sophia raised an eyebrow, clearly unconvinced. She turned in her seat to sweep her gaze over the sparsely popu-lated room. "You should've picked a busier night, then. It's quiet midweek. Especially since we opened so recently."

Kasia tugged at the brim of her hat. "Fine." She took a sip of her drink, hiding behind the glass. "Maybe I was taking you up on your offer."

Without asking, Sophia slipped a cigarette from the pack in front of Kasia. She held it to her mouth with one hand and gestured for Kasia to light it with the other. Kasia obliged, unable to look away from Sophia's pursed lips as she did. "We've piqued your curiosity, then?"

"You've piqued my curiosity," Kasia said. The boldness of her own words surprised her. Immediately, she tried to temper it. "When we spoke at your house, I realized how much this place means to you. It sounded like a dream you've had for years."

"It is," Sophia said. She rested the fingers of her free hand against her other arm.

"Why?" Kasia asked. "It's hard enough running a speakeasy. You've got to dodge the cops and the morality brigade just for selling liquor. There's money in it, but only if you can float yourself early and if you're lucky. You run a pansy club. It's another target on your back. A bigger, brighter target. Even people who don't mind the gin might want to see you shut down just for the customers you serve. The money can't be worth the trouble."

Sophia ran the tip of her thumb over the end of her

cigarette. "Why do you deliver for the Purples? Isn't it just as much potential for trouble?"

"The money is good, and guaranteed. Not like running a bar."

"That's the only reason?"

Kasia was silent. It wasn't the only reason, but it was the only reasonable justification she had. She'd wanted to make something of herself. She'd wanted freedom. She'd wanted respect. Running the Hamtramck Gang gave her all of it.

When she didn't respond, Sophia continued. "This is a place where people like me can live openly, just for a little while. We dance with who we want to dance with. We drink, kiss, talk, love, without looking over our shoulders. We meet friends and then we care for and protect one another. We'll always find each other and create new spaces for ourselves. It's an honor for me to do it. It's worth every risk."

Sophia's expression was set into hard determination. But she spoke with a warmth and fervor that caught Kasia in a whirlwind. She was passionate, certainly. But there was something else. "That's the only reason?" She repeated Sophia's words back to her.

The woman stared at the burning end of her cigarette. After a moment, she turned back to Kasia. "When I fell in love with Regina...." Sophia bit her lip, her brows furrowing, calculating her words. "Especially after my husband died...." She took a long drag before continuing. "I'd always felt different, but I did my damndest to hide it. I threw myself into doing exactly the things I was supposed to. Now I had a name for what I was, I didn't know how to live like that anymore."

Sophia flicked the end of her cigarette with her thumbnail. "My parents would institutionalize me if they knew.

And of course, there was always the risk of prison if I were caught. I felt completely alone, and so wrong—like I'd been made from faulty parts."

Kasia looked at her lap, her breath caught in her throat. She didn't see Sophia place her hand on her shoulder, and the touch was startling.

"A couple women from the hospital put two and two together, with Regina and I. And instead of telling my secret, they showed me that there were people like me— places for us. When I found those places... it was like coming back to life."

Kasia dared a glance at Sophia's face. It was unexpectedly serene. Hesitantly, Kasia asked, "What do you mean, coming back to life?"

"Why don't you come meet my friends?" Sophia said. "I think you'll find it easier to understand that way."

"No, no," Kasia said, waving her away. "I don't want to interrupt."

Sophia slid down from the stool. She reached for Kasia's hand. The press of Sophia's skin against her palm sent lightning through her. "You aren't interrupting. I told you, it's what we do. Come on." Her voice held a stubbornness that Kasia was sure she couldn't fight. Even if she could, with Sophia holding her hand, Kasia would let herself be led anywhere.

Sophia leaned in close to Kasia, whispering in her ear. "You can introduce yourself however you'd like," she said. "They won't pry like I did. Not when they're just getting to know you." She squeezed Kasia's hand, and it felt like an embrace. "You don't need to worry about them accepting you. You're with me, and that's enough for them to know you're alright."

With Sophia. *With* Sophia. The thought sent a thrill down Kasia's spine.

Sophia sat them at the head of the table. Three had been pushed together to accommodate her crowd of friends. She raised her voice to cut through the chatter. "Everyone, I have someone I'd like you to meet." The noise died down a little, everyone turning to examine Kasia. Despite Sophia's reassurance, Kasia squirmed from their attention.

It took a moment of awkward silence to realize that Sophia was waiting for her to introduce herself. "I'm Andrew," she blurted. Using her own name would make her feel too exposed, and she already felt naked enough.

True to her word, Sophia didn't bat an eye, and neither did the rest of the table. Sophia snaked her arm around Kasia's elbow and pointed to each person as she made introductions around the table.

The group was as mixed as Kasia had seen on the Lavender's busier nights. Sophia started with the two men closest to her, both in suits. "This is William, a dear friend in town from Chicago. He's here with George, who I've just had the pleasure of meeting myself."

Next, Sophia pointed to a handsome brown-skinned man in bohemian clothing. "This is Paul. He runs the Starlight in Black Bottom, but he's been so kind as to take a night off to visit. And hopefully give me some pointers."

"Oh, you're doing fine," Paul said, though the compliment made him glow.

"When I've got crowds like you do on a Wednesday night, I'll be doing fine," Sophia said. She gestured to the woman next to Paul, her luminous mahogany skin perfectly complimented by a yellow tea dress. "This is Louise. She performs at the Starlight and I'm hoping she'll make an appearance on the Lavender's stage."

"Keep the drinks coming and maybe you'll get a song out of me," Louise joked. Her voice was lower than Kasia expected. She realized that, just as she hadn't been born an Andrew, Louise might not have been named Louise at birth. Even if their reasons were different, as Kasia suspected they were, her presence was comforting. The small, secret voice in Kasia seemed to rise up to meet her. It whispered hope that it meant, just maybe, that Sophia's friends might understand her.

Sophia's next introduction interrupted her thoughts. "This is Florence and Annie." Florence had a soft, bronzed face and wore a dashing suit that Kasia couldn't help but envy. Florence seemed to size her up and approve, raising a glass in greeting. Annie, beside her with an arm around the back of Florence's chair, gave Kasia a welcoming smile. While she looked nothing like Sophia—she had blonde, straight hair and even sitting was clearly a tall woman—she reminded Kasia of her all the same. It was something about her queen-like bearing. Later, Kasia was unsurprised to learn that Annie modeled for local fashion shows.

The introductions went on around the table. Clara, "like Clara Bow," with huge, soulful eyes to match the comparison. Walter and Willy, Mildred and Lilly, Herbert and Ida. The names swam around Kasia's head, trying to attach to the proper faces. Genders sometimes confused her, but she soon learned to follow the lead of introductions and passing pronouns and to simply accept them as they came. She suspected the group did the same for her. Part of her was curious, wanted to ask everyone about themselves, as if they could provide explanations and a home for her own feelings. But it seemed rude, having just met them, to dig into what for her was too deeply personal to discuss even with her closest confidants, much less near-strangers.

After the awkwardness of introductions passed, the group resumed their conversation, taking Kasia along with them for the ride. She couldn't understand some of the conversations, laden with coded queer terms she'd never heard. Violets, jockers, rough trade, basketeering. Others she'd heard before; "bulldagger" was commonly thrown around about Maude Hogan, and while she'd only heard "fairy" pejoratively, it seemed to have another positive connotation here. Sometimes, if she looked lost enough, Sophia would lean in to translate. The feeling of Sophia's breath on her cheek, her lips almost brushing Kasia's skin, made displaying her ignorance worth it.

The conversation moved fast, but Sophia's friends included Kasia as much as possible, even when she was confused. They delighted in bringing her in on queer secrets and personal histories. Even if she had little to say, she rarely felt left out. In what felt like no time at all, she was laughing—longer and harder and more freely than she had in years. Since Andrew left for the war, really. They bought her drinks, and she returned the favor. They'd raised a glass to her deliveries making their drinks possible. When their eyes swept across the group, they included her in their broad smiles. And they didn't seem to censor themselves around her; they spoke openly about themselves, the people they loved, the places they frequented. It was a trust Kasia couldn't return, and it filled her with strange regret.

Sophia seemed to sense it. Her hand alighted on Kasia's knee. Suddenly, Kasia couldn't hear the table's chatter or the clink of glasses behind the bar. Every sense focused to the neat point where Sophia's body connected to hers. She could feel the heat of her hand—or was that only what she wanted to feel?—and the gentle pressure of her touch. Sophia's nails were red, with bare half-moon crescents at the base. The color against Kasia's dark trousers was a shock, an awakening, sudden color in her gray world.

"You can let your hair down here, you know," Sophia murmured. "If you want."

Her voice startled Kasia like she'd been woken from a dream. "What?"

"We all wear a mask out there. We have to. That's why places like the Lavender exist. So we have somewhere to take it off."

Kasia's face burned. She hid it behind a swig of her drink. She'd downed four glasses of liquor in quick succession. Her head was swimming. "I don't think I know how to be without it," she admitted.

"That's okay too." Sophia squeezed her thigh, and Kasia thought her heart might stop.

And then her hand was gone, and Kasia could hardly stop herself from grabbing for it. She wanted to press Sophia's palm against hers, feel the interlacing of their fingers. If there was anywhere she could do it, it should be here, in a room free of the judgment she feared. But she was still. The inches between their hands felt insurmountable.

She'd spent the rest of the night agonizing about her inability to close the space between them. Even the joy of the crowd that swept up Kasia in its raucous, messy tenderness couldn't drive the thought from her completely. She couldn't stop sneaking glances at Sophia's delicate hand on her lap, and the foot of space between them. Her own hand would twitch, stretch, begin a tentative journey forward. And then she'd catch herself, bringing her hand back firmly and torturously into her own lap. When Kasia finally went home, late enough that the night was just barely giving in to the first light of day, Kasia slept restlessly. Every time she woke, her failure was her first conscious thought.

As she blearily sipped tea the next morning and replayed the night in her mind, though, other feelings came. The soft hum of exhilaration, the taste of freedom. Deep loneliness, and at the same time, a feeling that she wasn't alone after all. A sense of acceptance. The sound of a call, a summons, booming deep in her marrow. Fear that she was inadequate to answer it.

The blend was a pleasant agony. She carried it with her through her morning, chewing on it, despite the contorted feelings the thoughts evoked.

# Chapter Twenty-One

Kasia's pleasant agony was disrupted by Officer Ward's frantic knock at the warehouse door. He entered without waiting for a response. In a few quick strides, he was in front of Kasia's desk, throwing an envelope in front of her. "I got your list," he growled.

Considering she'd just been lingering over the memory of Sophia's hand on her leg, Ward's intrusion made her want to punch him square in the nose. She took a deep, steadying breath and sat back in her chair, tipping her hat up to look the policeman in the face. "Good morning to you, too."

Officer Ward scowled. "I held up my end of the deal. We're done. And you won't tell my wife."

Kasia shrugged, reaching into her jacket for cash. She counted out a few dollars and held them out between her fingers. The officer stared down at it like he wanted to spit on her hand. But he took her offering and shoved it into his pocket. "I gave you my word," Kasia said. "But I still expect you to behave like a gentleman." She leaned over the desk on crossed arms. "I'll keep my mouth shut about you as long as you keep your mouth shut about me."

The officer turned his back on her. Instinct prickled in her stomach, rose the hair on the back of her neck. Being done with her was one thing; not taking her seriously was dangerous. Dangerous for her, because without a bribe or a threat to reign him in, Ward might not mind his loose lips. And dangerous for Ward, because she'd have to retaliate.

Before he could leave, she called his name. He paused, but didn't turn around to face her. "When your wife finds out, it probably won't be me. She'll find out because you're sloppy. You don't have the good sense to keep your secret woman a secret. Stop bragging around and showing her off. If your wife doesn't know yet, it's because she doesn't want to. You're not half as smart as you think you are."

Officer Ward looked at her over his shoulder. She could see the fire in his eyes, the set, low brow and the tension in his jaw. It thrilled her. "That makes two of us, you fucking deviant."

Rage tore through her. He'd handed her the excuse she was looking for. Ward needed to be reminded of the consequences for crossing her. Kasia leaped over the desk, sending her ledger flying. Ward turned, and she slammed into his chest, arm wrapping around his neck, and dragged him to the floor. She crushed his sternum under her knee, freeing her knife from her boot with one hand and grabbing his hair with the other. She tilted his head back and pressed the metal against his neck. A thin ribbon of blood unfurled beneath the blade.

"I'm smart enough not to antagonize a man more willing to resort to violence than I am," Kasia said. "You can't say the same."

"Andrew?" Stan's voice was timid. Kasia didn't even

know Stan had come in. She glanced up. Behind Stan, Czeslaw's aunt who ran the front desk was staring with wide eyes and an open mouth. She turned and fled back to the safety of the front room. *That* was intelligence.

Kasia stood, releasing Officer Ward. She offered a hand to help him up. He ignored it and forced himself unsteadily back to his feet. "Do we understand each other?" she asked. Officer Ward nodded, adjusting his uniform with a child-like pout. "Good. Get out of here."

Stan and Kasia watched the officer leave. Her friend looked dazed. "The fuck are you doing, Andrew?" he said. "That was a cop you just assaulted."

Kasia shrugged. "That was *my* cop I assaulted. He won't say anything. He just needed a reminder." She retrieved her ledger and the envelope from the floor. Sitting on the edge of the desk, she opened the envelope with the knife still in her hand. "You came at the right time. Ward just dropped off Harding's hit list."

"Oh?" Stan crept towards her. He seemed wary of getting too close. "Any of ours?"

Kasia scanned the list. The first few weren't in her territory. The next two were. And the sixth—

The sixth was the Lavender.

# Chapter Twenty-Two

Kasia sent Stan and Henry to warn the proprietors of their bars on Officer Ward's list. The Lavender, she would handle herself.

The drive there was agonizing. One second, she was longing to see Sophia again. She pictured her at the desk in her small office, offering her a cheeky smile. The next she dreaded it, knowing she wasn't delivering good news. Her whole body worked to shake out the agitation that filled it, fingers drumming against the steering wheel, foot tapping an uneven rhythm, head rolling out the tension in her neck.

The Lavender was quiet except for the clunk of the printing press echoing from the floor above. James hummed out of tune while polishing glasses behind the bar. They exchanged nods. "Sophia here, or are you by yourself?" Kasia asked.

"She's out until tonight. Where are your friends? Hard to carry our order down by yourself. I'm not much for heavy lifting when stairs are involved."

Kasia felt the wind go out of her sails at Sophia's absence. But there was no time to waste on disappointment.

"About that." Kasia threw her hat on the countertop and ran a hand over her face. "I have it on good authority that your joint's on a hit list. There's a raid coming. I don't know when," she added as James opened his mouth. "But you need to prepare like it's tonight."

She could read every feeling on James' face as he took in the news. Disbelief, panic, contemplation. "We've only just opened," James said, as if time could protect them. Kasia let him process it, a long silence passing between them. "We've got boxes of bottles in the back," he said finally. "We can store them at Sophia's. She's got room."

"No." Kasia shook her head. "You don't want them anywhere connected to the two of you. I'll stash them somewhere instead."

James shot her a hard glare. "They've already been paid for. We aren't going to pay to get them back, or some kind of bullshit storage fee. We can handle this ourselves. In fact, believe it or not, we've prepared for this possibility."

Kasia sighed, knocking her fist twice against the bar. The tinkle of shaking glasses cut James off. He glared again. Something told her that James required a softer approach than she was naturally inclined to take. "No repurchase, no storage fees. This is an offer from the kindness of my heart. And with all due respect..." she took a seat on one of the stools and clasped her hands together. "We've got a police chief on a mission. You could use the help. Anyone could. I'm offering it." She jerked a thumb at the office door. "You don't just need to get the bottles out. You need to remove any ledgers or paperwork that even hints at what this place is."

"Of course," James said, sounding aggravated. Kasia pressed on anyway.

"Any glasses or cocktail ingredients or anything that

can't be explained away by offering lemonade. You rent from the place above you, right? Talk to whoever's in charge. You need to get a cover story watertight."

"Officially, we're a private tea club run by the newspaper upstairs," James said.

"Perfect. Let them know what's coming. Make sure you're on the same page about every detail. How long you've operated. How many members. Topics of discussion. Events you've held and on which dates. You need *everything* to align. Anything in here that doesn't scream 'tea room' needs to go."

James knitted his brows. "I've run a dozen gin joints. I know how to prepare for a raid."

"Of course. I don't mean to insult you. I'm offering another set of hands. You just said you didn't like carrying things on stairs."

"I've got a bad back," James said defensively. After a long moment, he released a sigh. "Alright. Come with me. I'll pull out everything that needs to go from the back. You get it all out of here. I'll go upstairs and talk with the paper."

"I'll pack up anything from the front that needs moving, too. I'd rather get it all in one trip. If you've got eyes on you, every ride back-and-forth raises suspicion." Kasia stood and threw her jacket onto the stool before rolling up her sleeves in a few crisp motions. "Let's go."

# Chapter Twenty-Three

The raids hit two nights later. Three of Kasia's clubs that hadn't made it to Officer Ward's list fell. With the proprietors sitting in jail, there was every chance her name came up in interrogations. Usually, they knew better than to name names. They didn't need the Purples on them as well as the cops, and they often planned to reopen after paying fines and displaying brief public repentance. But Chief Harding clearly planned on pushing harder than his predecessors. There was no telling what he'd threaten or offer to confirm his suspicions.

Her work required her to always look over her shoulder, but this new level of diligence and paranoia wore her down. Clubs closing meant less work on her plate, but the free time did her no favors. She avoided the warehouse, with operational security as her excuse. The real reason was that she'd rather brood in her own home, without having to wash dust out of her hair.

Kasia knew she should lie low. Maybe even skip town for a while, just to let the heat die down. Visit the lakes or catch a train to Chicago. She hadn't had a day off in a decade. She could take some space from Detroit, clear her head. Or maybe just disappear. She could find work as Andrew—another factory job, or maybe she'd just bus tables at a restaurant. Something that didn't put a target on her back. Something quiet.

She'd dreamed of running away as a girl, but after her change into Andrew, she never thought she'd dream of leaving the Hamtramck Gang behind. She'd expected to seriously contemplate another life even less. Kasia had spent a decade wanting so few things, most of which she'd gotten. She couldn't abandon it all after coming so far.

It was overwhelming, though, how much she wanted something different for herself. She couldn't picture what. But wasn't it the perfect opportunity—or at least good enough—to find out?

She knew what she wanted to do. Should do, even, for her own safety. She also knew why she wasn't doing it. Sophia.

Sam wouldn't be happy with the raids. Even though Kasia had sent word of the bars on the list outside her territory, he'd be baying for Harding's blood. There was no telling what he might do to get it. Leaving Detroit and Sophia behind meant leaving her exposed to Sam's wrath.

Kasia hadn't seen Sophia since her last visit to the Lavender. It haunted her, the feeling of an unfinished moment. Sophia was every other thought she had. The thrumming heat of her body when she was close. The soft, red plump of her lips. The scent of her skin, like warm, sweet bread, beneath her perfume.

Inevitably, she ended up at Sophia's door. Kasia couldn't escape her pull, as surely as if she'd been leashed. She climbed the porch steps a thousand times in her mind before her feet ever hit them. Her knock echoed exactly as it had in her head. The maid opened the door, just as she imagined. Her mouth formed the words like she read from a script. "Good afternoon. Andrew Kasowski. I don't have an appointment, but I'm hoping Sophia will see me anyway. It's urgent."

"Mr. Kasowski," the maid replied. "Ms. Worley has been expecting you. Please, come in."

Kasia felt her heart crawling up the back of her throat. No matter how many times she'd rehearsed this mentally, nothing prepared her for the feeling of standing in Sophia's foyer again. Just as nothing prepared her to see James with Sophia in her study.

"Andrew," Sophia said. Sophia crossed the room to grab her hands. "We owe you an enormous debt of gratitude."

It was almost impossible for Kasia to hear her. She was too focused on the feeling of Sophia's palms against hers, the gentle press of her fingers into Kasia's skin. Kasia shook herself off. James was here, which meant by necessity, this visit was as much business as pleasure. "No, no. We always let customers know if we hear about a raid coming. It's part of the job."

Over Sophia's shoulder, James gave Kasia a knowing look. Kasia stepped back and tugged at her jacket, clearing her throat. Sophia sat again at her desk and gestured towards a chair next to James on the other side. Just like the Lavender's small office, the desk was cluttered, piled with books and papers. Once Kasia sat, Sophia continued. "It ensured that no one was there to arrest. That, in itself, was enough."

"The Lavender made it through unscathed?"

"Not quite," James said. "The cops trashed the place looking for evidence. They didn't find anything, but they took it out on us. Chairs and tables smashed. They cut open the stage platform with a saw. Hell, even the bar is cracked."

"It's a message," Sophia said softly. James and Kasia watched her fold her hands and rest her chin against them. "From Harding. He's not protecting me anymore."

"What do you mean?" Kasia prodded. *This is it*, she thought. *This is what I've been waiting for.* It made her feel strangely guilty.

Sophia's knuckles were white. Her face showed she was making extensive calculations before she spoke. "His wife and I.... We were involved. For a short while. And I convinced her to contribute to the Lavender. She sent me money in secret. His money. Then she brought me to their summer house, and he caught us. She confessed everything, even about the money. He was up for chief, the worst time for a scandal. I leveraged it a little. Not for much. A gentleman's agreement, silence for the right to be left alone." Sophia caught her lip between her teeth. "He's done paying for my silence."

Kasia was quiet. It was exactly what she needed to know. What Sam would want to know. The information that would make her a Purple. She should have felt triumphant. Instead, all she felt was terrified. Sophia wasn't just in danger from Sam. Harding wasn't going after the Lavender out of moral fervor—he had a grudge to settle.

"Then we take it away," James said. "We go to reporters, he's removed, he's not our problem anymore."

"No." Sophia shook her head. "It's a last resort. It takes me out with him."

James frowned. "Everyone knows who you are, Sophia. What, it's said out loud instead of in whispers?"

And then how do I support myself, much less help *you* support a business?"

"Wait," Kasia interrupted. "What do you mean, support yourself?"

James raised a brow at Sophia. "You haven't explained your little scheme?"

"It's not a scheme," Sophia said. "It's just soliciting donations."

"And before you had the Lavender for them to donate to?" James said.

"They were still contributing to the Lavender. Just not directly. You know how hard I've worked to make this possible."

Kasia cut in again. "I don't understand. Soliciting donations from who?"

James said, "Half the women in high society."

"Oh, it's not half, and you know it," Sophia snapped. "Besides, *you're* one to talk."

"I don't convince the men I sleep with to give me money for my company."

"Maybe you should, and I wouldn't be the only one floating the Lavender."

Kasia blinked, mouth dropping open. "You're a call girl?"

Sophia eyed Kasia for a moment, her expression somewhere between anger and concern. She shot James a glare before responding, "More like a courtesan."

Kasia looked around. "I thought you got by on your late husband's money."

"Money runs out," Sophia said. Her face was set in determination now. "And I knew that if I wanted the Lavender, I needed more than I had."

Kasia was too stunned to think. After a decade in her line of work, she'd met plenty of streetwalkers and good-time girls. She'd never been a client, at least not the traditional sort—but they always had useful information, and she was happy to pay for it. For all the derision she'd heard from the men around her about their profession, she understood. Better than most. You did what you had to do when survival was on the line. You also did what you had to do if you wanted to afford a little comfort. Living hand to mouth might be living, but it was a hard living. She'd made her own choice to take on greater risk in service of a little dignity for her and her mother. Sophia being a—courtesan, was that the word she used? —was shocking because Kasia would never have expected it, and didn't understand how Sophia was finding female clients. She'd never heard of women soliciting sex before. But if Sophia found a market for it, that was just good business.

The more Kasia thought of it, the more she had to admire it. She'd thought Sophia had been handed a jackpot in her late husband's estate. And maybe she had, if she'd sat back and enjoyed the freedoms afforded a moneyed widow before the next husband came along. But she'd worked hard and found her own way for the sake of the Lavender. It wasn't just another gin joint. She knew now why Sophia thought it was so important. And If there was one thing Kasia understood, it was making the most of the hand you were dealt.

By the time she started listening to the conversation again, James was back on going to the press. "It's practically free advertising for you, isn't it?"

"Don't be a pig," Sophia snapped.

It was a quick reminder of the rest of the world's view on Sophia's work. She was in more danger than Kasia had realized. She slammed her fist against the desk, sending papers toppling. James and Sophia jumped, startled into silence. "Sophia going public with this puts a target on her back. Not just with the cops. With every single person like Harding who has something to lose if she talks. Not to mention every religious fanatic and queer-hater with a pistol and an anger problem." She was nearly shouting. "We go through every other option. Any other option. It's off the table."

"And what other option springs to mind?" James said sourly.

"I've got time and resources to find one," Kasia shot back. "And a working brain."

"Excuse me." Sophia's voice cut between them, low and firm. "I'm right here. And I'm inclined to agree with Andrew. We don't have to respond right away. We need a few days to think."

James threw his head back and sighed. "Fine. And what about the club in the meantime?"

"Start over," Kasia said. "You need a new spot and a new name."

"But no one was there during the raid," Sophia protested. "Why would we need to start over?"

"Because they're waiting for that," Kasia said. "Harding included you on that list because it was personal. He's not going to let this go just because you got away the first time. If you want to do this, you're a silent backer. There's no way around it."

"I suppose there isn't," James conceded. "Which means the Lavender is dead."

The word hung in the air around them. Sophia's eyes grew damp, her mouth quivering against threatening tears. Kasia fought the urge to catch Sophia's cheeks in her hands. She wanted to throw her arms around her and hold her so tightly it could keep Sophia's shattered pieces in place. But Sophia stood and shooed them away. "That's enough of all this. We're not going to get anything figured out today. I need to lie down."

James stood. "We need to discuss how we're going to finance a new club."

Sophia gave him a look of disbelief. "*Later*, James." Sophia said, already walking through the study doors.

Kasia and James eyed each other. James reached into a pocket, revealing an impeccably polished silver cigarette case and lighter. He pulled out a cigarette and offered the open case to Kasia. "Thanks," she mumbled. James flicked open the lighter, presenting the flame.

"I sounded like a real ass just now," James admitted. He lit his own cigarette.

"You sounded ungrateful to the woman floating your business," Kasia retorted. "Where I'm from, that's not how you talk to the person signing your checks." She tapped her cigarette against a glass ashtray on the desk, more aggressively than she meant to.

"I've known Sophia a long time. We met in the war. Fast friends," James said. "And we've seen a lot together since then." He worried the end of his cigarette with this thumb. "To be honest, I wouldn't mind her doing the work she does—if it wasn't *her*. I told her this would happen. The wrong person learns what she's doing, and she's sunk."

"You mean you're sunk," Kasia said. "Because she's funding you."

James sat in the chair beside her, pulling it around so they could be face to face. "Look. The Lavender was always Sophia's dream, not mine. I can always find a job running another blind pig. I've been doing it for years. Running Sophia's made me happy. She's a good friend, and I wasn't going to turn down an opportunity to help her out. But getting herself tangled up with rich people and their money... it was never going to end well."

James took another drag of his cigarette before continuing. "One thing you should know about Sophia," James said finally. "She never backs down from a fight, but she runs from an argument."

Kasia crossed her arms, glaring over the lit cigarette in her hand. "What makes you say that?"

He tapped his own cigarette against the ashtray. "I've seen many lovers come and go with her." James's tone was pointed. "She doesn't keep anyone around long. Just a bit of resistance, and she's ready to go. I'm not talking about her work, either. We're business partners, and we argue, but I always say the only reason she's kept me around is because neither of us wants to fuck each other." He cocked his head. "I like you, Andrew. You're a good man who's done right by us. I owe you a favor, and this is the favor I'll do you. Don't get attached to Sophia Worley. She can't help herself. She'll break your heart."

# Chapter Twenty-Four

At home, her mother was waiting for Kasia in the kitchen. The hanging light above the table cast deep shadows beneath Gosia's eyes. She clenched her hands in front of her, fingers red and knuckles white. Kasia froze in the doorway.

"There's been police here, asking about you," Gosia said. Her voice was thin.

Kasia ran a hand over her mouth. Her eyes narrowed on her mother. "What did you tell them?"

"They asked for letters from my daughter in Chicago. I didn't have any letters to show them."

Kasia sighed. "None of them have kids that don't write?"

Her mother glared. "They asked about Andrew. They asked me how it felt to have my son...." She caught a sob in her throat and swallowed it. "How it felt to have my son back." Gosia shook her head, her eyes fixed on the table. "Then they told me about the company you've been keeping behind my back. Gangsters. *Inverts.*" Kasia paled, her heart dropping to her feet. She knew Harding had been watching her. She didn't realize he'd been watching so closely.

Gosia wiped her cheeks with a wrinkled handkerchief. "You're not my son. You're not my sweet boy. You brought police into this house, and shame on our family. You've destroyed your brother's name."

Kasia took a step into the room. "You didn't seem to think I was bringing us shame when I kept a roof over your head. And food in your mouth." She leaned against the table, looming over her mother. "You knew *exactly* what I was doing, and you never said a word. You kept quiet while I broke my back getting established so you could retire." She tore off her jacket. Anger—years of it—rushed to the surface. "You never even said my name, Mama. You've never called me Kasia again. You never spoke up about what was happening. And now, suddenly you've got shame? Why, because you can't close your eyes and pretend I'm Andrew? You can't pretend he came back from the war and runs financials for a paper supplier? It was all fake, and you knew it. You just preferred the lie."

Gosia was silent. She raised her head to meet Kasia's gaze. "My son is gone," Gosia said finally. "And so is my daughter. You, some kind of demon—you've taken them both." She stood, and a rosary dropped from her grip. It hung between them like a ward. "Leave my house." Kasia hesitated, and Gosia raised her voice. "I said, leave!"

"I paid this house off," Kasia growled. Her mother stood firm, nearly a foot shorter than her daughter, head tilted back to hold her gaze. Kasia stalked to her room, throwing whatever important personal effects she could think of into a bag. Her mother was still in the kitchen when she left, murmuring rapid prayers.

A closet in the back of the warehouse held a flimsy cot with a rough blanket. It wasn't the first time an irate mother or wife kicked someone in the gang out. The cot was uncomfortable, and the warehouse was often loud and busy, but it provided a roof overhead for anyone who needed a night away from home. Or several nights. Kasia wasn't sure how long it would take her mother to reconsider. She wasn't even sure if she wanted to go back home in the first place. Now that everything they hadn't been saying was said, there was no putting it back. She stared, dejected, at the lumpy mattress. The possibility of sleeping on it indefinitely was too grim to contemplate.

Despite the late hour, Stan was the first person to find her. He paused in the doorway to the back room, brows raised. "Andy. Is that your bag on the cot?"

Kasia bit back a sigh. She should've closed the closet door. "Lots of pressure on us lately. Staying away was smarter, but it's easier to keep on top of things here," she lied. "Anything from Sam?"

"I was just about to leave you a note." He held out a piece of paper.

Kasia glanced at the writing. It was so cramped and smeared that she could barely make out the words *Sam called. Meet tomorrow.* "What is this? What did he say? Where am I meeting him and when?"

"Oh." Stan thought for a moment. "Uh, he didn't say why. He said not to meet at the deli because it's been compromised. I think he said the Joe Muer Oyster Bar."

"You think?" Kasia flopped down onto the cot, throwing one arm over her eyes. She was exhausted enough without having to puzzle out what Sam wanted her to do because Stan wasn't any good at note-taking.

"Pretty sure. At, uh, 6:30 tomorrow," he added helpfully.

Kasia sighed. "Thanks. Go home, Stan, and turn off the lights behind you."

"Will do."

The light clicked off, leaving Kasia alone in thick layers of dark and silence. She knew she should sleep; the warehouse crew for the actual paper supplies would be in and working by 5:30 the next morning. But Kasia couldn't stop ruminating on the conversation with her mother, or on what Harding might do next. For that matter, she had no idea what to do about Sophia. James's words still rang in her ears. She knew she should listen. Sophia Worley was trouble. She'd been distracted when her boys needed her at her best. The cops' intrusion on her mother was proof of that. And now that she had the information she needed, Kasia didn't *have* to spend time with Sophia at all. But she couldn't stop thinking of Sophia's face when James said that the Lavender was dead. Her sadness was unbearable. The memory trampled wild and reckless over Kasia's other concerns.

She always had a plan, clear next steps, anticipation of every possible outcome. This time, her thoughts were shapeless. The future seemed like an endless loop of a black frame on a film reel. Maybe Sam would let her handle Harding, and keep Sophia safe in the process. But if she figured out how to pin down Harding and forcibly remove his attention from the Purples, Sophia, and Kasia herself—what then? What about the next chief, or the one after that? She'd never be able to operate her business in peace. Hell, she'd never expected to. Kasia knew from the beginning that her job had a shelf life. It never crossed her mind that she wouldn't go down for it at some point. But she'd never questioned whether it was worth the outcome until now. She wondered whether Sophia would spare her a visit or two in prison.

# Chapter Twenty-Five

The oyster bar was hopping. Kasia never thought much of oysters; they looked congealed to her, a wad of pale, shapeless flesh floating in ocean brine. The fine people of Detroit clearly didn't share her opinion. They sat shoulder-to-shoulder in booths and on barstools, eager to pick through the half-shells on icy trays.

Sam sat in the back, nursing a drink. Kasia took a seat across from him, nodding her hello. Sam got right to it. "I assume you've been keeping up with the news?" Kasia nodded again. "Making it hard to do business. Lots of eyes on us." Kasia didn't bother to point out that she'd warned him about those eyes before the trouble became apparent. He took a measured swig from his glass. "Now would be a good time to tell me your luck panned out with Harding's friend."

A chill grabbed Kasia's spine. Once Sam knew about Sophia, she wouldn't have a choice about whether to use the cards she held. Sam would make that decision for her, and he wouldn't care whether Sophia herself was the cost. But if he found out Kasia was withholding information—information that could keep the Purple Gang, and her own, in business—she'd be out on her ass, if she had an ass to be out on. Sam wasn't forgiving. All the goodwill she'd built with him could fall as easily as knocking over a castle made of cards. Kasia's thoughts scrambled for a way to split the difference. "Harding doesn't think much of whatever she has. He raided her bar."

Sam leaned back in the booth, checking over his shoulder before continuing. "You're not thinking this through, kid." He leaned back in, voice lowering. "He could be trying to scare her into silence. Or he could be betting that the information is just as harmful to her, and he's testing her willingness to follow through with consequences. What's your read on it?"

"*My* read on it?" Sam was spot-on, but she couldn't tell him that. Not if she wanted to keep Sophia safe.

Kasia was stalling for time, and Sam looked irritated. "Yeah, kid. Your read on the situation. Why's she holding back if he broke his end of the bargain?"

There was no good answer. Nothing that got her out cleanly, at least. "I don't know. Maybe she's still figuring out what to do."

"Jesus Christ. What have you spent your time on her for, then?" Sam pulled an ashtray closer with an ear-shattering clatter. "You've been fucking around for weeks with this broad. Get me the information I need. You can't get her to say what she's afraid of? Give her a reason. Make her fear you more than him if you have to." He'd pulled a cigarette from the case, and was waving it, unlit, as he gesticulated. "It's your own life on the line, kid. Always. Now more than ever."

Sam paused to light his cigarette. His lighter flickered and died. Sam fiddled with it, hit the spark wheel again twice, but no flame came. Kasia offered her own, opening the top and flicking it on before holding it out to Sam. The man let out a long exhale through his nose, lit up, and passed the lighter back. His face was set now, the fury in his brow easing back into contemplation. "You need to know," he said, "what's coming. Two delivery teams are down. Full teams, not runners. Police followed them back to headquarters and ambushed them. Bodies stacked on bodies. Good men and bad. The ones that made it out intact are sitting in jail, but maybe not for long. Depends on how well they can keep their mouths shut."

Sam tapped his cigarette lightly against the ashtray. His mouth twisted up into a grimaced smile. "I don't want you to be one of them." He rapped his knuckles against the table. "You're smart, usually. You've got a lot of piss and vinegar in you, but you know how to lead. Even better, you know how to plan. You've got more patience in you than you think. You're useful, and I don't want my investment in you to go to waste." He locked eyes with Kasia. "You understand me?"

Kasia nodded. "I get it. You're fond of me."

Sam barked a laugh. He shook a pointed finger at her. "Don't get ahead of yourself." Sam took a drag of his cigarette and continued. "What I'm saying is, it's your time. A better place in our organization. Officially, not a contract. And that's a promise." Kasia couldn't help it. She knew Sam was dangling bait, but her heart raced anyway. "But the catch is: you have to *live* in order to get it. Preferably outside of a jailhouse." He tilted his head. "And you know how you can do that?"

*Betray Sophia.* "You want to know what information Sophia Worley has," Kasia said.

"That's right." Sam raised an eyebrow. "This is it, kid.

It's for real. You tell me what Sophia Worley has on Harding, and you're a Purple. So, anything else you remember that might be helpful?"

It would be so easy. She could tell Sam everything, and it would be out of her hands. What he did with it was up to Sam. Maybe her problems with Harding would disappear. Her stomach tightened when she remembered that she'd also be brought into the Purple Gang. Part of the family. A step she wasn't sure she'd ever get to take.

Sophia's story would no longer be hers to tell. She'd be at Sam's mercy then, just as much as Harding. Kasia swallowed. "No." Sam held her gaze, unblinking. "But I'll get what you need."

Sam's face fell, full of disappointment. It was almost worse than her mother's. Kasia fought the urge to win his approval back. It would say too much, and he wouldn't respect it, anyway.

He sighed and patted her shoulder. "Good." He waved a hand, dismissing her. "Of course you will. Don't take too long and don't go easy."

# Chapter Twenty-Six

The warehouse was the last place Kasia was going to be able to think her way out of this. The crowded back room suffocated with heat and noise. Only Joe was silent, glowering with his back to the wall. Kasia glanced around—every member of the Hamtramck Gang was present. "What's going on here? You have your assignments." She motioned for Stan to get out of her desk chair and collapsed into it the second he stood. "It's not Friday yet." At least, she was pretty sure it wasn't Friday. The days were blurring together.

"You heard about the delivery busts?" Pete said.

Kasia waved him off. "Of course I heard."

"Well?" Stevie said. "What do we do about it?"

"You make your deliveries, like you're contracted to," Kasia said. Voices competed over one another, the angry shouts blending into white noise. Kasia yelled over them. "We'll move the trucks and paint over them. Until then, don't go your usual routes, and don't come back here when you're done. Park in a neighborhood somewhere and walk home. I don't want anyone here unless you absolutely have to be. Including right now."

"And what if we don't?" Joe's voice cut through the rest. The gang fell silent. "You want us to keep working on a sinking ship? Doesn't matter how tight the mainsail is, boss. We're taking on water too fast."

The guys murmured their agreement. "Sam's pockets are full enough," Ludwig said.

"I can't blame you for wanting out," Kasia said. Her voice was low, and the room quieted to hear her. "I thought about hopping a train a few days ago." She picked up a pen from her desk and fidgeted it between her fingers. "But I'm still here. Do you know why?" She pointed at Stevie, and he shook his head. "Czeslaw?" he shook his head as well. "Because I have a duty to all of you." She gave Joe a particularly pointed look. "I can pull us through this. I can take care of Harding. If I can do that, we're all still employed and out of prison. That's if Sam knows we're reliable."

"And if you pull off whatever bullshit you have planned before we're caught in the next bust," Stan said.

"Yes," Kasia acquiesced. "That's why I need you all to keep a clear head and look after each other. Keep each other safe by keeping your distance. Change routines. We can get through this. Sam promised us more money and work at the other end of it. But I'm not making anyone do a job they don't want." It was a half-lie. He'd promised Kasia a promotion, not the Hamtramck Gang. But she'd always intended to bring her boys up with her.

Kasia stood. "Anyone who doesn't want to work for me anymore is free to go. Just know that if your stomach for this job goes bad now, you're not getting hired back when the pressure is off. No hard feelings. I'd never say a single word against any of you boys. You go live your life. The factories are shutting down left and right after the crash, but whatever work you can find, you find it. You can even come to me if you need a dollar to get through the end of the month. Just don't ask me to come back." No one moved. "Well? Anyone I need to give my well-wishes to?"

Joe stood and left, slamming the door on his way out. "Good luck to Joe," Kasia said, and turned her attention back to the rest of her crew. "Anyone else?"

Silence answered her. "Great. Now get out of here."

# Chapter Twenty-Seven

The sun made a spectacular appearance for Kasia's next delivery. Pickup from the Purple Gang had moved to a farm outside of town. It wasn't the time of year for idyllic natural surroundings. The grass around the barn was brown, peeking up in spots through melted snow. But while the wind still bit through her coat, the edge of the bitter cold had softened. Spring was slipping a few tentative tendrils into the year. Kasia wanted to lie in a sunbeam like an overindulged cat. She had a flash of an image, her head in Sophia's lap, cradled between her legs in some sun-strewn meadow. Kasia shook off the warmth that spread through her, embarrassed. She wasn't a daydreamer. Especially not now, when her job demanded more attention than ever.

Stan, Henry, and Kasia lined up between the barn and the truck, passing boxes of liquor between them. The truck no longer advertised paper supplies on the side and instead boasted full linen services. It had been difficult to finagle getting it repainted in a week, but money and calling a couple favors in won the day. Their customers knew to expect new delivery times and days. She'd mapped out new routes for each delivery, trailing through private neighborhoods or intersections so busy it was easy to get lost in the traffic. Nothing made them safe, Kasia knew that, but she'd taken every step she could to protect her crew.

They worked in silence, familiar with the rhythm. Even on the road, when the boys usually cut up to pass the time, Henry and Stan were quiet. Henry drove, with Kasia in the passenger seat with a marked-up map, and Stan between them. Kasia directed turns, and in between her instructions they stared, tense-faced, out the windows.

The first three deliveries came and went. If their customers were more concerned about being caught than usual, they didn't show it. The routine of carrying in the boxes, taking money, and discussing the next order was all the same. The tension in Henry and Stan eased, lulled by familiarity.

In the truck on their way to the next stop, Stan grabbed Henry's hat and flipped it in his hands. "Oh boy, Har. This new?" He peered into the hat and let out a low whistle when he caught a glance of the label. "This is where all your money goes, huh?"

"Give that back." Henry grabbed for his hat, eyes still pinned to the road and missing entirely.

Stan put the hat on himself and turned to Kasia, pointing at it. "What do you think, Andy?"

Kasia shrugged. "Looks better on Henry." Henry's father had been a tailor, and it showed in the care he took with every detail of his clothes. Stan was rumpled on a good day. On a bad one, he was downright slobby. The crisp felt of the hat only offset his stained shirt and sagging pants, barely held in place by his suspenders.

Henry finally grabbed the hat back with a snort. "How a

man presents himself is important, Stan. You might have more luck with women if you didn't look like you crawled out of a puddle in a ditch."

"Nah," Kasia said, "he'd have to keep his mouth shut, and that'll never happen."

Stan feigned offense, resting a hand on his chest. "I do just fine when I don't have a steady gal. Suzie doesn't mind me, anyway. She does my laundry, so she knows it's all clean. She'd rather I spend my money to take her out."

"A lid for every pot, you lucky son of a bitch," Henry said. "Hang on to that one. You might never find one again. You'll be a filthy, banged-up pot out here with the rest of us lidless and blue saps." He parked and jerked his thumb towards the back. "Let's get this done quick, like the boss likes it." He threw a wink in Kasia's direction.

It was never a long stop for them—a small speakeasy, hardly bigger than a poor man's kitchen. Only a few boxes of liquor. They each carried one in. Then it was back to the truck. One more delivery, and they'd be done. Kasia checked the lock on the back and froze.

She felt a prickle in her neck. Slowly, she turned her head, scanning for anything that gave her pause. Two men in plain suits walking towards them from one direction, another two from the opposite way. Moving too quickly.

Kasia ran to the passenger door and swung herself inside. "Go," she hissed to Henry. He hit the gas, and they pulled out into the street. A police car turned and followed from an alley. "Shit," Kasia murmured. "Shit, shit, shit." Another police car joined them. And another. Henry kept his foot on the gas pedal, weaving between honking cars as they gained speed. Kasia pulled her pistol from her coat pocket and checked the bullets. Fully loaded. That was something.

Stan held his own gun at the ready. Henry concentrated on the road in front of them, squinting into the light. "If we can't lose them, run. No one in the same direction," Kasia said. The sound of the sirens nearly covered her words until gunfire cut through.

They all ducked together, synchronized instinct. Bullets tore into the back of the truck. Somehow, all three were unhit. Kasia suspected their luck wouldn't hold. She leaned out of the passenger window and fired back towards the police cars in two quick shots. She had no idea if either made their target before she dove back inside, just in time before the cops returned fire.

There was a deafening pop. The truck swerved, scraping the side of parked cars on the street. Kasia and the boys slammed against each other and the dashboard like rag dolls. The truck crashed to a halt, the engine squealing.

Kasia wasted no time. "Get out, run," she yelled. Her door was smashed in, with a sliver of light visible where it used to meet the cab body. A couple of hard kicks opened it just enough to slip out. The right side of her body ached, and blood filled her mouth. There was no time to wonder how much damage had been done. She took off towards a side street, adrenaline pushing her steps faster.

Another round of gunfire. She heard a whistle near her head. And then a scream—guttural in a way that took hold of her and shook her. Every instinct said to turn and look, to see if one of her boys was hit. Kasia fought it and kept running.

A shot rang out. Almost as soon as she heard it, she felt something rip through her shoulder. She didn't feel pain at first. Just an intense heat, like she'd been seared with a brand, her flesh left smoldering. Kasia gagged, resisting every urge to stop. More shots—a little more distant now.

She didn't dare stop running. She weaved between houses, jumped smaller fences. The neighborhood was a blur. She had no idea how long she ran, or where she'd run to. Her shoulder radiated with pain now. The sight of a shed in someone's backyard finally stopped her. She had to rest.

Kasia wrenched open the shed door and closed it carefully behind her. She sank onto the hard dirt floor. There was hardly room for her in the packed shed. It smelled of mold and rust. She was cold where the blood had soaked through her shirt and jacket. Her breath came in huge gulps, even as she rested her head against the wood wall.

She had to make it to nightfall. Easier to avoid the light than to stay inconspicuous in the day while covered in blood. And then she could... do what, exactly? Go to the hospital? Even if, by some miracle, the police weren't looking for her there, she imagined being treated for a bullet wound meant she'd have to take off her clothes. They'd learn quickly that she wasn't actually Andrew Kasowski. She wasn't sure what can of worms that would open, but she knew distinctly that she'd like it to stay closed.

Kasia shivered. She knew where she *wanted* to go. But going to Sophia's put her at risk. Sophia had enough problems without harboring a fugitive. Kasia thought she might be turned away at the door. Or worse, brought in, nursed and cared for, only to bring Harding down on Sophia's head.

She had until sunset to decide.

# Chapter Twenty-Eight

Finding her way to Sophia's house took hours. At least that's what it felt like. Kasia's shoulder throbbed. Her ribs ached with every step. Hair matted with blood hung in her eyes. She wasn't sure what had happened to her hat, but she suspected she lost it when the truck crashed. The sight of Sophia's porch filled her with both relief and dread. Each step required an almost insurmountable effort to climb, hauling herself up with a death grip on the railing. Then, finally, she stood in front of the red-painted door.

She raised a fist to knock. Kasia froze and let her hand fall. Being here was insanity. Putting Sophia at further risk was unimaginable. Her heart pounded in her throat. She turned away from the door, resting the back of her head against it. It sent a shock of pain through her neck—another injury she'd yet to discover.

Maybe she could get back to the warehouse. It was the last place she should be; the first place cops would look for her. But she could call someone for help. Sam, maybe? She doubted Sam wanted to get involved. But surely he'd send someone. Unless he didn't, and she was stuck on the cot in the back room waiting for the police to arrive.

Kasia was freezing. And strangely wet. Not from blood; the bleeding had mostly stopped. She realized she must be soaking in sweat. She took a shuffling step away from the door, and then another. Her legs shook and threatened to collapse.

There was no way she was making it to the warehouse.

Reluctantly, Kasia turned back around. She knocked, so weakly even she could hardly hear it. She tried again, harder. Her legs were buckling. Her knocks became frantic. The door swung open. She only glimpsed Magda's wide eyes as she fell.

The next thing she noticed was a returning sear in her shoulder. Her eyes opened. For a moment, she couldn't remember where she was or how she got there. The unfamiliar room only extended her confusion. Then she turned her head. Inches away from her face, Sophia dabbed the wound with a cloth coated in something that smelled strong and antiseptic. Kasia jumped, and Sophia laid a steady hand on her other shoulder and hushed her softly. "You're just grazed, but it needs cleaning." To Kasia, the chunk missing from the top of her shoulder looked worse than a graze. But Sophia's voice, low and gentle, was soothing. "We're nearly done."

Kasia tried to relax into the bed. Sophia's nearness made it almost impossible. Her burgundy silk robe slipped against Kasia's arm as Sophia dabbed the wound. Kasia focused on the feeling of it, cold and sensuous, to distract herself from the pain. Sophia finally stood, taking a tray covered in bandages and bottles with her.

She was at the door by the time Kasia could murmur a "thank you." Sophia paused only long enough to reply with a gentle *hmm* in return. Low voices slipped in from the hallway, too muffled to understand. Kasia closed her eyes. It was almost like being a child, when her father was still alive, and her parents' voices would float from the kitchen to the bed she and Andrew shared when they were young. She could almost feel him, warm beside her; the safety of his presence and her mother and father's vigil in the other room.

Footsteps interrupted her memory. When she opened her eyes, Sophia had returned. This time, she held a steaming ceramic bowl and washcloth in her hands. Sophia offered a tentative smile. "I've cleaned your wounds, but I thought you might like the rest of you a little cleaner as well."

Kasia flushed. She was suddenly aware that she was naked from the waist up. What was on her bottom half, she didn't know, but by feel she suspected loose pajama pants. Even though the blankets covered her up to her shoulders, it was the most exposed she'd been in another's presence in over a decade.

Sophia let out a small, low laugh. "I can leave this here with you, if you prefer. Would you like me to at least clean your face?" Kasia hesitated, then nodded. Sophia sat gingerly next to her and placed the bowl on the blocky bedside table. She dipped the towel and wrung it out. Her hands had surprising strength for looking so delicate. Kasia tensed as Sophia placed the warm cloth against her skin. She grazed the washcloth across Kasia's forehead, down her temple and to the edge of her jaw. The gentle heat spread through Kasia, her muscles loosening. The ache in her neck throbbed a little softer. Sophia dipped and wrung the washcloth again, then ran the cloth over the other side of Kasia's face, carefully avoiding the cut on her forehead. Kasia longed for the feeling of the cloth as soon as Sophia raised her hand.

The next pass was over her nose and cheeks. Sophia was rougher now, scrubbing blood from the creases of her nose. Kasia was unbothered. The scrape of cloth against her skin was a welcome intermediary of Sophia's touch. Another round of the washcloth around her mouth and chin. Sophia hummed under her breath, something that sounded like a jazz swing that Kasia couldn't quite place.

"Your neck?" Sophia asked. Kasia stared at her blankly. "You have quite a bit of dried blood on your neck. Can I take care of it?" Kasia nodded again, and Sophia swept the cloth in clean strokes from her neck to her collarbone. Her fingers brushed against Kasia's skin, sending a shiver through her.

Sophia set the cloth in the bowl. "There. I can leave the rest to you." Without a single thought, Kasia's hand shot out, gripping tightly around Sophia's wrist. Sophia jumped, her golden green eyes locking on Kasia's. After a moment, she melted back into her seat on the bed. "Something else you need?" She leaned in, hovering over Kasia. Her voice was barely above a whisper.

Kasia brought Sophia's hand to her cheek and pressed her palm against her face. Sophia's thumb moved in slow strokes across her cheekbone. Kasia leaned into Sophia's firm hand, eyes closing as she settled against it.

Sophia brushed a lock of hair from Kasia's forehead. The touch seemed to pull Kasia down into something warm and dark. Primordial. It washed over her in a wave. As it pulled back, the tide brought her with it into sleep.

# Chapter Twenty-Nine

When she woke again, it was to the sound of bustling and clinking dishes. Magda was setting down a tray with a bowl on her bedside table. Sun streamed into the room, warming it along with the roaring fire in the hearth. "You're up," the maid said as she glanced at Kasia's half-open eyes. "You should eat a little."

Kasia tried to push herself upright. Her ribs protested the movement. Magda caught her beneath her good shoulder and helped sit her up. "There," Magda said. She moved the tray into Kasia's lap. "Chicken soup. My mother's recipe."

"Thank you," Kasia said. Her voice was hoarse. Magda watched her closely as she dipped her spoon into the broth and sipped it. It could use more salt, but pointing it out seemed rude. "Delicious," she said instead, to Magda's approval. She'd never looked very hard at Magda before. She'd always thought Magda was pretty, but up close, Kasia could appreciate the fineness of her face behind the woman's sternness and the determined lines around her eyes and mouth. Her blonde hair was streaked with streams of grey, and her large blue eyes were set in a round face with plump cheeks.

Magda adjusted her pillows and pulled the covers straight. "Ms. Worley sent a client home when you showed up last night," she said. Was that a hint of mischievousness in her voice? She'd seemed so humorless to Kasia. "I've never seen her do that before. Well, once or twice. But it's very unusual."

Kasia took another polite sip of broth. "Well, a bleeding person collapsing on your doorstep is a mood-killer."

"Mmm." Magda sounded unconvinced. "Eat up. I'll come back for the bowl in a bit."

Kasia did as she was told, despite the lack of salt. She had no idea how long it had been since she'd eaten. She'd no sooner put the tray aside than the door swung open again.

Sophia entered with an armful of books. Her hair was clean and unstyled, her curls tucked behind her ears. It was the first time that Kasia had seen her bare-faced, and it certainly took nothing from Sophia's beauty. She wore a simple cream shift dress with an open sweater knit in chunky blue yarn thrown on top of it. It wasn't the glamor that Kasia was accustomed to seeing her in, but it suited her just as well.

Just as she had the night before, Sophia settled onto the edge of the bed. "I thought you might be feeling bored. Or you will be soon, after you've had more rest." She sat the pile of books next to her. "I didn't know what you liked, so I picked a few."

The books filled Kasia with dread. She pinned her eyes on her blanket. "Thanks. I'm, uh... not much of a reader."

Sophia slumped a little. "Oh?" She sorted through the stack. "You don't like books?"

"Books are fine," Kasia said. The thought that she'd disappointed Sophia twisted in her chest. "I just don't like reading."

"Ah. I see," Sophia said. She seemed to perk back up. "What if I read to you instead?"

Heat crept up the back of Kasia's neck. "Alright."

Sophia held up a book. "Have you heard of this?" she asked. "*The Well of Loneliness*. It was banned in Britain a couple years ago for obscenity." She raised her eyebrows. "'Unnatural practices' between women."

"I've never heard of it," Kasia said. "But if you like it, I want to hear it."

"Haven't read it yet," Sophia said. "We'll figure out if we like it together." She opened the book to the first page and began reading. "Not very far from Upton-on-Severn— between it, in fact, and the Malvern hills...." Kasia already thought that Sophia's voice was lovely, but reading brought out a further depth and warmth in her tone. Kasia leaned into it, bathing in the sound of her words. She was hardly listening to what they were; the rise and fall of her voice, the quick little breaths she took between sentences, and the vibration of her chest were enough. Her mother had read to her as a child, and it always made her feel safe. This was different. Safe, yes, and warm; but the sound of Sophia reading also made her heart feel as though it would break through her chest. The words themselves might crack her open.

She fought the urge to doze. Kasia clung to the moment. She never thought she'd be here, in Sophia's bed, watching the way her curls framed her face as she read. Kasia tried to imprint into her memory how the light hit Sophia's cheek. The back of Kasia's hand rested against Sophia's sweater, draped over her thigh. She stroked the sweater with the back of her fingertips. It felt rough against her skin.

Sophia must have seen her struggling to stay awake. She came to a stop and closed the book. "You need rest."

"No," Kasia protested. "I'm fine."

"I'll read more to you later." Sophia smiled, but her tone brooked no argument. Kasia relented and slid down into bed, wincing as her bruised ribs protested. Sophia looked satisfied.

"Thank you," Kasia said. "You didn't owe me this much."

"No," Sophia said. "I didn't." She bit her lip. In a movement so quick Kasia almost missed it, she leaned in and brushed a kiss over Kasia's forehead. Before Kasia could react, Sophia was out of the room, the door shut behind her. The books laid with Kasia in bed.

Kasia couldn't help but grin. For the first time, it was Sophia who was flustered. It was almost as good as the kiss.

# Chapter Thirty

The next few days blurred with sleep, punctuated by visits from Magda with meals and Sophia to read to her. It was the longest Kasia could remember being still. She hated the moments she woke without Sophia or Magda around. It was always the same— a brief moment of peace, sunk deeply into the mattress, the smell of Sophia's perfume still lingering; then a shattering feeling once she remembered why she was there. She thought of Henry and Stan, every memory twisting her heart into shameful, tangled knots. Their steady loyalty led them into the shootout. She prayed they'd escaped. The possibility they hadn't haunted her.

The only time she felt any relief was when Sophia visited. Sophia hardly even allowed her to sit up unaided. The woman was always in a flurry of activity—fluffing pillows, adjusting blankets, tying the curtains up or taking them down, tidying the bedside table. It was a welcome distraction. The only time she sat still with Kasia was when she read.

It was one of these moments, halfway through *The Well*

*of Loneliness,* when Kasia dared to take one of her hands from the pages. Sophia stopped mid-sentence, staring down with surprise. "Can I ask you something?" Kasia said. Sophia nodded. "Something Magda said after I got here.... She said you'd sent home a client when I came. Did she mean...?"

Sophia went pale, her gaze running along the patterns in the blanket. After a moment, she raised her head to look Kasia in the eye. "Yes."

Kasia kept Sophia's hand in hers, running her thumb along the back of it. "I didn't know women sought that kind of thing out."

Sophia shifted in her seat on the bed. Her shoulders relaxed a little. "I don't know that they do. But some women —women with means, who need discretion even more than most—are glad to find it."

Kasia pulled herself upright, wincing as she moved. "But if they know what you do, how do they remain discreet?"

"We're all surrounded by a polite fiction," Sophia said. "I can be written off as a close friend. Those who know, know because they've done the same. Men are harder that way. Men coming in and out of my house is harder to explain. And they brag to their friends."

"You see men as well?"

Sophia shrugged. "I don't prefer it, but money comes faster and easier that way. When I've really needed it... well, I've done what I've had to." She searched Kasia's face as if looking for her challenge, for judgment, and found none. Sophia tilted her head. "Do you think of me differently?"

"No." Kasia felt awkward, unsure of what the proper

etiquette was in this unusual situation, but she knew that much. "Do you? Seeing me like this?"

Sophia laughed, startled. "You're asking if I see you differently because you're injured?"

"No, not exactly." Kasia reddened, struggling to put together her thoughts. "But... until recently, you only knew me as Andrew. Now you know. You knew I was hiding, and now I'm hiding all over again, but in your house. It's not fair to you. You know I'm weak, and I've made it your problem."

Sophia was quiet as she considered Kasia's words. Kasia's heart hammered against the dozens of possibilities of what Sophia might say.

"Do you remember what I told you at the Lavender?" Sophia said finally.

Kasia flushed. "Yes," she said. "I remember everything."

"We all wear masks," Sophia said, echoing her words from the week before. "Sometimes to hide, and sometimes as armor. Sometimes, the mask is all artifice. And sometimes, the mask is part of us—a little, at least, just as much as we're allowed to show. Just enough to wear a little piece of ourselves that's real, that we can find the joy of ourselves in. It isn't weakness. It's the will to live. It lets us survive. It's the only thing that lets us survive, sometimes. Hopefully long enough to find people who don't need a mask to accept us." She squeezed Kasia's hand. "So, no, I don't think of you differently. Instead, it's an honor to meet you, Kasia, with masks off."

After her brother left for the war, Kasia forgot what it was to be understood. It was like being flayed open, organs laid bare to the world. Uncomfortable. Visible. And somehow, at the same time, it was the solid, loving heat of a hearth, her body whole and languid in front of it. Sophia saw her vulnerability and chose to protect her.

What could she say to that? What words were enough? Kasia could think of nothing. Instead, she raised Sophia's hand to her lips and placed a kiss on the back of it, like she remembered knights doing in fairytales. "It's an honor to meet you, Sophia."

Sophia's cheeks flushed. For the second time, Kasia had flustered her, and it felt so good that she wanted to do it over and over again. She would spend a lifetime trying to make Sophia blush.

The woman squeezed her hand again. "Are you tired?" Her voice was huskier than normal, thick with something unspoken. Kasia shook her head, but her drooping eyes betrayed her lie.

Sophia smiled and kissed her cheek. Kasia's eyes closed as she drank in the press of her lips to her skin. "Get some rest," Sophia said. "I'll read more to you later."

# Chapter Thirty-One

Kasia called a Hamtramck Gang meeting the moment she left Sophia's. A week had passed, but the warehouse was still too dangerous for Kasia to ask her boys to meet her there. Her pain had improved, but she didn't want to test how well she was healing with another run from the law. Her bruised ribs and stiff neck meant she was moving slower than usual. She didn't particularly want to see the gang after what happened. Or rather, for them to see her. But she had a responsibility to them, and waiting would be a show of weakness.

They met in Ludwig's kitchen, in a home nearly identical to Kasia's. A grim silence permeated as they filtered in. They hardly even offered each other a hello. The boys took seats at the kitchen table while Kasia stood with her back to the counter. She would really prefer to be sitting. Still healing, she tired easily. But she'd rather they not know.

Czeslaw and Stevie watched her with a slack, unreadable faces; Ludwig and Pete looked anywhere else. Kasia took a deep breath. "Okay. Update me on Henry and Stan."

Stevie's face contorted. There was a long silence before he replied. "They're dead, Andrew," Stevie said. Pete put his head in his hands. "Stan is, at least. Henry's in the hospital, but it looks like he's not far behind."

"You missed Stan's funeral," Czeslaw said, not bothering to disguise his bitterness.

Kasia had suspected as much. But the confirmation tore through her like a bullet, a dark, sick feeling that hollowed her out. Reflexively, she performed the sign of the cross, her head hung. Tears stung her eyes. She thought of Stan's grieving girlfriend, the light of his life, dressed in black by his coffin. She thought of Henry's gentle, steady affection, his acceptance of her rivaled only by Sophia's. She thought of them cutting up in the truck, hard-working and playful in equal measure. All of her memories flooded her at once. She reeled, struggling to stay on her feet. But she also thought of Andrew, how badly she wanted to collapse with her mother when the letter came. Instead, she'd helped her mother to bed. Kasia had duties to attend to. Just like before, those duties kept her standing.

"I'll move money to their families," Kasia said, her voice cracking. She cleared her throat. "To help with expenses."

"I doubt their families want to hear from you," Ludwig said. "You're the reason they're dead, Andy."

The rest of the boys turned to look at her. Their faces telegraphed a potent combination of hatred and fear. "It's the right thing to do," Kasia said. She squeezed her eyes shut, trying to block out their stares. "I understand why they don't want to see me. Someone else can deliver the money. But it has to be done."

"Who?" Pete said. "We're done, Andrew. It's too much. You were supposed to keep us safe."

The hollowness in her stomach was an excellent

furnace for anger. It flamed through her, turning her cheeks red. "I never promised safety. I promised money. None of this was ever safe, and you all knew it. I did my best to protect you. This isn't a job with a pension. You die, you get arrested, or you get very lucky over and over until you aren't anymore."

"We shouldn't have trusted you," Czeslaw muttered. "You're a fucking invert." A different kind of silence overtook the room. "We all know it," Czeslaw said. "You show up in Andrew's clothes and step into his life, fine. People do all kinds of things to get by. You proved yourself in the neighborhood, you got us a contract with the Purples. You made yourself useful. But the second you noticed that pansy club bitch, you've been distracted. I'm starting to think you're only after your own sick kicks, *Kasia*, and fuck the rest of us."

"You should think real hard about what you're saying, Czeslaw," Kasia warned. She felt the pull of the knife tucked inside her boot. Early on, if anyone implied how convenient it was for Andrew to show back up just as "Kasia" moved to Chicago, it was the fastest way to get them to keep their suspicions to themselves. But she'd lost two friends already. Despite the flame inside her, she couldn't bring herself to harm another one. "I've looked after all of you in the best way I can. I gave you opportunities you'd never have had otherwise." She looked at Ludwig. "You have this house because of me," Kasia said. Then, turning to Pete, "You couldn't keep a job for more than a week before I found you." She gripped the edge of the counter behind her. "You think I'd do all of this just to fuck a woman?"

"No," Ludwig said quietly. "I don't. But I think whatever you've got wrong with you, it's going to take us down." Kasia stiffened. "You've spent all this time obsessing over

Sophia and what she knows. We could have gotten ahead of this faster without you. You always take risks, but once you met her you've been all impulse, no forethought." If only he knew exactly how much thought preceded her every move. Kasia had to admit impulse might be driving her decisions more than usual, but lack of thought wasn't the problem. "A pretty cunt can take down even the best men," Ludwig said pointedly. "But if you're in that position, you can't lead."

"What are you talking about?" Kasia snapped. "Every one of you has gotten caught up in a girl before. More than once. I've never heard any of you say Sam shouldn't be where he is in the Purples because he's got a mistress."

"Sam's where he is because he can keep whatever he's got going on to the side," Pete said. "You can't. Not from what I've seen."

"We told you, we're out," Stevie said.

Czeslaw nodded. "You've done a lot for us. You're right about that. And we're grateful—I am, anyway. But we can't trust you anymore." He glanced at the other guys at the table, as if gathering strength. "We voted while you were gone. We've got no confidence in you, Andy. We're moving on."

Kasia felt her fury turn into a crushing weight that left her cold. "Fine." She sniffed and ran a hand over her face. "But the contract with Sam is through me. You won't be working for him anymore."

"Sam's a sinking ship," Pete said. "If you want to be a drowning rat, that's up to you."

There was nothing else to say. With her hands shoved in her pockets, she left. She'd lost her crew, and there was no time to mourn it yet. There was too much else to fix.

# Chapter Thirty-Two

Kasia hadn't expected to be back on Sophia's doorstep so quickly, but it was the only place that she wanted to be. Magda let her in immediately, and Sophia was close behind. She searched Kasia's face, taking in her slumped shoulders and drawn face. Sophia cupped Kasia's cheeks in her hands, her eyes wide as she looked up at her. "What happened?"

Kasia leaned her forehead against Sophia's. If she stayed just like this—if she could inhale Sophia's scent, feel her warm skin against her face—she could shut out everything else. But Sophia pulled back, her expression full of questions. Kasia shook her head. "Henry and Stan are dead."

Sophia gripped her arm. "Oh, Kasia. I'm so sorry."

Kasia fought her tears; admitting out loud that her friends were dead made it real. Struggling not to cry made her chest tighten. Her shame threatened to overwhelm her, to send her to her knees. "And the rest of the boys are out," Kasia continued. "With everything that's happened, they're running scared." It was easier than saying she'd let them down. That because of her, Henry and Stan were gone, and she'd lost their trust.

Sophia turned to the maid. "Magda, could you please bring tea into the sitting room?" She looped an arm through Kasia's and walked her to the swan-backed chaise. "Lay back," she ordered. Kasia rested her head against the sofa's curved arm, her legs sprawled out in front of her. Sophia sat next to her and laid a hand on her stomach, careful not to press against her bruised ribs.

Magda brought the tea, and Sophia passed her a cup. Kasia cradled it in her hands; the smell and steam alone felt strong and soothing. "I have no idea what to do," she admitted. "I've spent ten years chasing the same goal, and I've lost everything."

Sophia tilted her head. "Not everything," she said.

"Not quite everything," she conceded. "But I can't work without a delivery team. I'm not welcome in my mother's home. Sam's not interested if I'm useless to him." *And I am useless, because I can't imagine telling Sam about Sophia now,* she thought. "I've lost two friends, permanently. And I lost the rest, guys I played with on the street as a kid, because I was responsible for their deaths. I used to be a legend in my own neighborhood, and now I'm a disgrace." Kasia scowled. "Which means I've made Andrew a disgrace." It somehow bothered her most of all, that she'd dragged her brother's name into infamy. It wasn't a legacy he deserved. "And the worst part is, I always knew. I've never had any illusions that it would go any other way. If not now, then another ten years down the line."

Sophia's mouth opened and closed again. She bit her lip. "What is it you really want, Kasia?"

Kasia sat up slightly, hitting Sophia with a frown. "What do you mean? What I've always wanted. A crew of my own to run. Working for the Purples. Success. Money. Respect."

"Do you?" Sophia said. "Because what I see is a death wish."

Kasia snorted. "It's a job hazard, not an end goal."

Sophia brushed her fingers against Kasia's cheek. "Or maybe you feel ashamed of the choice you made to live in an identity closer to your own."

Kasia sat up. "What I chose was an income to support my mother with." She pulled away from Sophia, crossing her arms over her chest.

"And if you didn't have to support your mother," Sophia said, "what would you do?"

Kasia shook her head. "I don't know. I've never had a choice not to think about it."

Sophia ran her thumb along Kasia's chin. "Now you do."

Kasia's jaw jutted out, her teeth clenched tight. Maybe it was the anger and grief that roiled unrelentingly in her chest, but like a wounded animal, Kasia lashed out. "You don't know me. Not really." Her voice, already defensive, rose until it filled the room. "I'm doing exactly what I want, and I'm fucking good at it. What else is there for me? I can't work in an office. Half the people I know have been laid off from the factories. What do you want, that I live hand to mouth for the sake of feeling better about myself?"

Sophia withdrew her hand, clasping it in a fist on her lap. "I didn't say that." Her voice held a tight, defensive edge that Kasia had never heard from her before. "I suggested you think about other options that are less likely to end with you dead."

Kasia fought the urge to tear into Sophia. She wanted to tell her to fuck off and mind her own business. She wanted to ask if fucking for money was more what Sophia had in mind. She was a hypocrite to be lecturing Kasia about dangerous work. She bit her tongue and turned towards the back of the chaise. "I need to rest," she said under her breath. "And I don't need to be prodded by you like this."

"And I need to work," Sophia snarled, "because I've been looking after you for a week with no income, and I have a club to save and a community to serve." She stood and smoothed her dress before pulling her sweater tight around her waist. "Magda will bring you lunch. I suggest you eat."

"I can look after myself," Kasia said. She hated how pouty she sounded, like a petulant child.

"Then do that," Sophia said on her way out the door. "Find someplace else to go."

And then Kasia was alone. The sitting room was silent, save for the crackle of the fire in the hearth. Her anger cracked, and regret began seeping in at the seams. She wished she hadn't spoken that way to Sophia. She wished she'd done things differently, kept Henry and Stan safe. Kept the trust of her friends. The regret twisted, braiding itself with her shame. Kasia wanted to cry, but the weight of it all kept the tears from falling. She pressed her face into her hands, breathing in deep gulps. Wave after wave of shame, flaring from her gut through her chest and shoulders, locking her stiffly in place. Panic slipped through the waves, screaming questions about where she would go and what she would do.

It was like being locked alive inside a tomb. Unable to move, unsure how much time had passed. Magda's voice shocked her when it came, as though she'd broken the dark spell Kasia was under. "Lunch is ready," she said, startlingly close to Kasia. She hadn't even heard Magda enter the room. Kasia turned to look up at the maid, who was wearing a firm expression. "Come eat in the dining room, like a gentleman. I've fed you so many times and you've never sat to eat it properly."

The idea of eating was appalling to Kasia. Her empty stomach clenched at the thought. But another fight was even less appealing, and Magda looked like she wasn't in the mood to argue. Begrudgingly, Kasia turned and hauled herself to standing, unable to look the other woman in the eye.

Magda led her to the dining room. The maid had set out a sandwich, a cup of tea, and a small bowl of fruit. Kasia sat obediently and thanked Magda, who left her alone to eat. Everything tasted like ashes breaking apart in her mouth, and swallowing required decided effort. Her body, though, seemed to appreciate it. After she'd choked down half the sandwich and a bit of the fruit, she could feel herself settle. The guilt and shame were far from gone, but she broke through the sense of drowning in it, her head finally above water.

The hours ticked by. Kasia wandered from room to room, trying to stay out of Magda's way as she cleaned. Sophia's office drew her in. Bookshelves lined three walls, each stuffed full. Some even had books stacked in piles in front of those properly shelved. Kasia forced herself to read through the titles, her mouth moving as she struggled to decipher the words. Fiction, nonfiction, biographies, scientific references, classic titles she recognized, and far more that she didn't. She wondered if Sophia had read them all. She knew Sophia was a savvy woman. Her cleverness had always appealed to Kasia. But she was also clearly intelligent, or at least well-read. Somehow, it made her feel even worse about dismissing Sophia earlier.

Distracting herself in Sophia's office only worked in fits and starts. A pile of fashion catalogues on Sophia's desk reminded her of Henry. She wondered if he'd been right about wide trousers coming back into style. A book on mechanical physics reminded her of Stan, who liked tinkering with the delivery trucks. Every memory of them sent a shameful shock through her. She'd forget for a moment, drawn by something else to discover in the room, and then feel guilty for having thought of anything else when she remembered them again.

After losing her father and brother, Kasia thought she knew grief. She'd gotten good at pushing it aside. She'd never even cried for Andrew, no matter how much and how often she missed him. But now, whether it was her exhaustion or the pain that still ate at her, or whether it was all finally just too much to bear, she couldn't keep her grief at bay. She was standing in front of a shelf with her hand on a copy of *The Beautiful and the Damned* when it finally overwhelmed her.

Kasia fell to her knees. Grief, shame, and regret—sinking into them was like sinking deeper and deeper into the ocean, a suffocating pressure that stole her breath and crushed her body. Tears rushed into ragged sobs. Then a high, thin keening, ripped from her chest despite the thought in the back of her mind that Magda might hear and come to find her. She didn't want to be seen. She was sure she couldn't look another person in the face ever again.

Henry and Stan. Andrew. Her mother. Her friends. Sam. And now Sophia. All her work, all her planning, all her good intentions had only hurt the people she cared about. And there was nothing she could do about it but lie in a ball on her side, feeling the carpet bite into her cheek while she sobbed.

# Chapter Thirty-Three

It was well after dark when Sophia's voice rang through the house, announcing her return. Kasia had finally risen from the floor, empty and numb. The sound of Sophia's voice made her freeze from her seat in the office, where she'd chosen to sit and contemplate her options.

Sophia had told her to find somewhere else to go. Kasia wasn't sure she was even supposed to be there. She wondered if she could sneak out with no one noticing. Her thoughts were once again interrupted by Magda popping her head in the door. "Dinner will be in an hour," she announced. "After Ms. Worley finishes her bath." Kasia nodded. There was no leaving now. Well, she could, but that seemed unfathomably rude after Magda made it clear she was including her in her dinner plans.

And she wanted to see Sophia. She needed to apologize. Her anger was too much to bear on top of everything else. It clawed at Kasia's stomach.

Sophia emerged for dinner in the same robe that she wore the first time Kasia met her in her home. The ends of her hair were still damp, her curls hanging to a fine point around her face. Her cheeks and nose were pink and shiny from their scrubbing. Kasia's heart twisted as she watched her take her seat, her posture upright and graceful, the bearing of a queen.

Three places were set at the table. "Magda always joins me for dinner," Sophia explained as she followed Kasia's gaze. Kasia sat as Magda entered with three steaming plates piled with roast chicken, potatoes, and cooked spinach. She set a plate down in front of each of them.

They ate awkwardly at first, the only sound between them the soft scraping of utensils against plates. Sophia broke the silence first to ask Magda about her day, the progress of house tasks, and upcoming appointments. The conversation drifted into small talk, with light, occasional laughter coming from one woman or the other. Deeply familiar and comfortable. The room seemed to warm around Kasia. After her breakdown that afternoon, Kasia felt strange and out of place. But the comfort between the other women was intoxicating; she wanted so badly to slip into it. She waited for a pause to ask, "How did the two of you meet?"

Magda and Sophia exchanged glances; Sophia nodded encouragingly. "I met Ms. Worley at a speakeasy for a certain clientele," Magda said.

"A queer bar," Sophia clarified. "The Overture. Do you know it?"

Kasia shook her head. "Never heard of it." She felt her cheeks prickle in embarrassment at her ignorance.

"That's not surprising. It hasn't been around for a decade, and it was hardly the size of this room. Shoved between a hat shop and a tailor on a side street downtown." Sophia smiled wistfully at the memory. "We became fast friends. When I needed a maid with excellent discretion, she volunteered for the job." She looked affectionately at Magda.

Magda shook her head, but a smile lit her lined face. "I needed work, and Sophia offered it," she demurred. Her eyes cut to Kasia. "Ms. Worley, rather."

"I think we're all past pretense," Sophia said. "Magda is like family," she added to Kasia. "I wouldn't have it any other way."

Kasia felt jealousy stir in her chest. Not for Sophia's affection, or not exactly. But of the clear warmth between the two of them that permeated the room. Kasia loved her mother, but affection was never part of their relationship, at least since her father passed. She could still remember her mother drawing into herself; confusing and jarring for Kasia as a child. Her father was gone, and so was her mother, in a way—no embraces, no pecks on the cheek, no stroking her hair, not anymore. Andrew hadn't fared any better, but at least had the respite of their mother's continuous pride. Here, despite lacking the ties of blood, was a deeper connection than she'd come to associate with family.

Kasia smiled, and the two women continued. They reminisced about stories from their shared past, at turns gripping each other's shoulders with laughter. Kasia was silent, feeling as though she was outside of them and peering in longingly, but she was grateful for the change of atmosphere.

Magda cleared the table while Sophia led Kasia to the sitting room. Kasia's awkwardness returned. She found herself standing in front of the hearth, staring into the flame. Sophia lounged on a sofa behind her, propping her head up in her hands.

"I'm sorry for what I said earlier," Kasia said finally, gaze still firmly on the fire. "You didn't deserve that."

"It wasn't the right time for me to bring up my concerns, anyway," Sophia acceded. "I apologize." They were quiet for a moment before Sophia added, "Come here."

Kasia drifted to Sophia's side. Sophia moved her legs up so that Kasia could sit next to her. "With what you've been through lately..." Sophia stopped and caught Kasia's hand in her own. She seemed lost for words, her eyes on the couch between them.

Kasia was just as unsure what to say. Part of her wanted to explain everything, to tell Sophia every awful thought she'd had that afternoon. But she was her mother's daughter. She didn't discuss feelings. She didn't know how. Something in Sophia's averted gaze told her she understood, anyway, as best she knew how.

Sophia's eyes finally rose, anxiously searching Kasia's face. A question—fraught, but blessedly distracting—came to Kasia. "James said something to me," she said. "That you never run from a fight, but always run from an argument."

Sophia laughed. "Well, I suppose he knows me well enough."

"He also said you don't keep lovers long," Kasia said.

She expected Sophia to be angry. At least to protest. Instead, she looked into the fire while she squeezed Kasia's hand. "I haven't," she admitted.

Kasia's heart dropped. "Why haven't you?"

Sophia looked back at her, contemplative. "I've never wanted to lead on someone whose feelings are stronger than mine." She paused. "James falls in love like it's tripping on the curb. I don't fall so easily." She tucked a strand of hair behind her ear. "You look upset. Does it bother you?"

Kasia caught her bottom lip between her teeth. "No."

Sophia's half-smile returned. She sat up, closing the distance between them. "You're wondering how I feel about you."

Kasia suddenly felt shy. She wished she had her hat to hide behind. Sophia brushed the backs of her fingers against her cheek.

"I've grown quite fond of you," Sophia said. "Earlier... I should have waited to say what I did. But keeping you alive seemed more important."

"Have you?" Kasia felt a smile pull uncontrollably at her face. Tentatively, she offered a hand. Sophia took it and squeezed her palm.

Sophia pulled herself to sitting, closing the distance between them. "Terribly," she admitted. Kasia could feel Sophia's breath on her cheek as she whispered. The nervousness Kasia felt from Sophia's closeness flared, then was overtaken by something stronger, primal, something that ached and cried. It washed over her, overwhelming.

A flare of guilt for thinking of anything other than her lost friends rose. And then, a sudden understanding—the *need* for it. Instead of running, she let it come. She let herself fall into her need for Sophia, for closeness, for comfort. For the part of her that longed to be known. For the thought that she could lean on someone else instead of playing the pillar. She had nothing but the woman in front of her. Somewhere, deep in the crevices of her pain, lay an unexplored freedom. For the first time, there was nothing between her and what she wanted. Softness. Tenderness. Sophia.

Kasia leaned in and tentatively pressed her lips to Sophia's. The supple give of her lips made Kasia suck in a breath, a gentle shock. Sophia pulled back for no longer than a heartbeat, searching Kasia's face. But soon Sophia pushed into her harder, wrapping her arms around Kasia's neck, their bodies pressed close. Her tongue flicked against Kasia's lips, an invitation, and Kasia's lips parted to meet it.

Sophia moaned against Kasia's mouth. Kasia's hands found Sophia's thighs. She squeezed the flesh, desperate to fill her hands with her. Sophia swung a leg over Kasia's lap. Kasia felt her way up, pausing to feel her ass, her waist, her breasts, each sending her into a deeper frenzy. She had dreamed of this, but to live it was better than she could have imagined. She slid her hands around Sophia's delicate collarbones, the long lines of her neck. She reached Sophia's head and clasped it between her hands, deepening their kiss, hungry. Kasia hitched an arm around Sophia's waist. She needed her closer. She needed to feel all of her at once, and the impossibility of it drove her mad.

Sophia's hips rocked steadily over hers. Kasia threw back her head and groaned as the grinding pressure sent a thrill through her body. Sophia took advantage of her exposed neck, her mouth meeting the bare skin, teeth nipping at the surface. Kasia pulled Sophia into her harder, her arms flexing with tension, breath caught in her throat. Sophia pulled back, just slightly, and it filled Kasia with disappointment. It didn't last long. "Come with me," Sophia murmured. She stood and took Kasia's hand. Kasia followed; Sophia could have led her to her own execution and she wouldn't have protested. They climbed the stairs and entered the privacy of Sophia's bedroom, the door locked behind them.

Kasia froze, her desire interrupted by her realization that she had no experience beyond her fantasies. Sophia was experienced, sophisticated; Kasia couldn't imagine herself as anything but a disappointment. But Sophia seemed to read her face. She offered her half-smile—cheeky, reassuring. Sophia cupped Kasia's face and kissed her softly. "We won't do anything you don't want," she said, her voice low, both comforting and thrilling. "Tell me if you're uncomfortable; it won't hurt me." She placed a line of kisses down Kasia's neck. Kasia's eyes closed, the rush of blood to her core overriding her anxiety.

Sophia stepped back, unhooking the belt of her robe. She shrugged it off her shoulders, revealing her bare body beneath. The sight left Kasia light-headed. The lushness of her—undulating curve into curve, ripe and bright in the low light—tore Kasia down and rebuilt her anew. There was before Sophia, and after. She had discovered a new world.

Sophia stepped close again. The unrelenting softness of Sophia's skin drew her hands, nesting into the deep curve of her waist. Sophia unbuttoned Kasia's collar and drew it from her shirt, dropping it to the side. One by one, she unhooked each button of Kasia's shirt. The brush of her fingers made Kasia tremble. Sophia stripped her of it, then set to work on the bandage binding her breasts, a quick glance up at Kasia to confirm her comfort. Kasia nodded, her breath shallow and desperate. It fell to the side, and Sophia took in her naked chest. Any self-consciousness Kasia felt was overturned by the hungry look in Sophia's eyes, the satisfied smirk as she took in Kasia's body, so unlike her own. Kasia was thin, straight, and hard, in contrast to Sophia's plushness. But Sophia's look was deeply approving, hungry. She ran her hands down Kasia's chest.

Sophia paused at her small, swollen nipples, hard in the cool air. Kasia gasped as her fingers brushed against them. Gently, Sophia took one nipple between her fingers and squeezed. Kasia pulled her in unconsciously, desperate for more. Sophia obliged, her mouth moving to the pink bud, teasing it with her lips. When Kasia whined, she placed her mouth over it fully. Her tongue flicked against it, sending an electric shock from Kasia's chest through every inch of her limbs. When Kasia moaned, Sophia drew her in closer with one arm, her free hand moving to Kasia's other breast, squeezing the flesh.

Kasia's desperation peaked. She clutched Sophia harder, bent down to whisper in her ear. "Please," she begged. "Please. I want you."

A mischievous look played in Sophia's eyes. She unlatched Kasia's belt and trousers, sending them in a heap to the floor. "Show me," she commanded. "Lay down."

Kasia divested herself of her shoes and socks, as well as the crumpled remnants of her trousers. She laid back as she was told, suddenly self-conscious again. Sophia climbed over her on all fours, one hand sliding up the inside of Kasia's thigh. Her hand met Kasia's opening, and all thoughts were once again swept away. Her fingers slid over Kasia's wetness. She drew it up and over Kasia's burning nub. "Very good," she purred. Kasia gasped. The sensation was unlike anything she'd felt before. Her stomach clenched, pleasure tensing every muscle of her body. Her world narrowed to Sophia's fingers sliding over her clit. She moved slowly, teasingly. It was almost unbearable. "Please," Kasia gasped again.

"So greedy already," Sophia admonished. Her fingers circled, unrelenting, as slow as ever. "We've only just started."

Kasia grasped Sophia's arm, digging hard into her skin. "Please," she repeated. This time, Sophia obliged, just a little. She pressed against Kasia harder, the motion still steady.

"Fuck," Kasia bit out. It still wasn't enough. It didn't touch how badly she wanted Sophia. She grasped Sophia's hair, hard enough to tilt her head back. Sophia chuckled, a smile warming her face. "Please," Kasia said, harder, more need in the edges.

Sophia pressed harder again, this time quickening the circle of her hand. Kasia clenched at the bedspread beneath her, back arching as though a thread reached into her stomach and pulled her up by force. "Good," Sophia murmured. The ecstasy between Kasia's legs grew, hot and electric. It filled her completely, broke through the barrier of her skin. It radiated, drew every muscle tight. "Come for me, Kasia. Let me watch you come." Her words sent Kasia over the edge. Finally, it broke, and washed back through her in a tsunami. Kasia didn't notice the moan being ripped from her throat. She noticed nothing except euphoria coursing through her and the delectably satisfied look on Sophia's face.

Kasia fell back onto the mattress, panting. Sophia leaned forward to kiss her, tongues deep and intertwined. She pulled back and pressed her fingers to Kasia's lips. Kasia hesitated, but opened her mouth. Sophia's fingers slipped over her tongue. The taste was unexpected, but delicious; salted, lightly sweet, a little sharp. And then Sophia was gone, leaving Kasia grasping for her. She settled between Kasia's legs, dipping her head between them.

Kasia's clit was sore in the wake of her orgasm, and she wasn't sure she could stand to be touched. But when the tip of Sophia's tongue met her, flitting so gently against the bud, it sent her back into rapture. Sophia took her time, drawing her out. Her little laps were far apart, broken by pressing her lips into Kasia's thighs and nipping at the flesh. "You look so lovely," Sophia said. Kasia met her eyes, and Sophia brought her tongue again to the bottom of her mound. Kasia answered with a groan.

Sophia wound her back up tight, step by step, methodical, patient. Kasia felt the pressure in her build. Sophia slipped a fingertip between the folds of her pussy, teasing the opening. She pressed, just a little, and Kasia felt herself part. A flare of pain broke through the pleasure. Kasia winced. Sophia's hand immediately withdrew. "Too much, darling?" she asked, concern knitting her brow. Kasia nodded, hesitant. She didn't want Sophia to stop completely. She pulled her in to kiss her and pressed her forehead to the other woman's. Once again reading her thoughts, Sophia asked, "Did you enjoy everything before it?"

"Yes," Kasia breathed.

Sophia smiled. "And would you like more?"

"Yes."

Sophia's hand grazed her mound. "Say it," she demanded.

Kasia complied immediately. She would have done anything for Sophia to be back between her legs. "Please. Please, Sophia, I want you."

"Very good," Sophia praised. She settled back at the end of the bed, her mouth falling back to the peak of Kasia's slit. Her eager tongue worked the bud, pressed deeper into it as she clasped Kasia's ass. It didn't take Kasia long to return to her bliss. It built again and overtook her. Soon it crashed over her again, sending a warm wave over Sophia's waiting tongue.

Sophia laid next to her as Kasia tried to regain her breath. She traced her fingertips over Kasia's stomach. Kasia looked up at her, Sophia's round green eyes rimmed with black lashes, the perfect pout of her mouth. Adoration overwhelmed her. She lifted her head to trace her lips over Sophia's cheeks, a silent worship. Once she laid back again, she raised a hand to Sophia's breast. Wonderingly, she pressed into the flesh. It was both firm and yielding. Sophia cupped her hand over Kasia's and pressed it harder. Kasia felt the heat between her legs grow again.

Sophia guided her hand down her chest, over her ribs and stomach, over the top of her mound. The hair at her core ·was wet and sticky. She slid Kasia's fingers over the incredible wetness. The need in Kasia twisted. Sophia's hand slipped beneath hers. "Watch what I do," she ordered. Her fingertip parted her lips, spreading the molten liquid. She pressed it to her clit and moved her finger over it in light strokes. Kasia wanted to dive into her mouth-first, to ravish her. But she watched, captivated by the sight of Sophia's pleasure. She waited until Sophia once again led her hand to her. Kasia felt clumsy at first, like she couldn't understand the sensations under her fingers. But the hard nub under her hand responded to her efforts. Sophia threw her head back and groaned. "Faster," she commanded, and Kasia obeyed. Sophia's chest heaved, the curve of her breasts moving up and down as she ground into Kasia's hand.

Suddenly, she rose and grabbed Kasia's wrist. She pushed her hand down further. "I want you inside me." She gripped Kasia tighter. "Two fingers. In and out."

Kasia slid against Sophia's slit until she found her opening. She pressed, and was suddenly surrounded by heat, soft and wet and tight against her. Sophia cried out, and the sound sent Kasia into a frenzy. She pumped inside of her, ignoring the burn of her arm. In the sweetest moment of Kasia's life, she watched Sophia writhe in a dance that mirrored Kasia's own minutes ago. Sophia's pussy pulsed around her like a rapid heart. The rush of wetness that followed coated Kasia's hand past her knuckles.

Sophia pulled Kasia towards her and she finally, reluctantly, moved her hand from between the woman's legs, leaving Sophia shuddering. Sophia clasped Kasia's head to her chest. "You did very well," she murmured, running her fingers through Kasia's hair.

Kasia wrapped herself around the other woman. She felt a kiss brush the top of her head. Sophia's body hummed with warmth. Kasia felt an urge to close her eyes overtake her, but she was kept on the edge of sleep by the continued pulse between her legs.

There was before Sophia, and after. There was no turning back.

# Chapter Thirty-Four

The night was languid and endless. They slept and woke by turns, chatted about nothing, kissed, fucked. Kasia was lost at every moment in the tangle of their limbs and the pressure of Sophia's body. She forgot that a world existed around them.

Until the world came to the door.

It wasn't quite dawn when the first knock came. It bit through the grey morning, sharp-toothed and snarling. It sent them both scrambling for their discarded clothes. "Magda?" Sophia called. The knocking repeated, a series of demanding bangs.

Kasia knew that sound. That was a cop-knock.

She grabbed Sophia's waist, spinning her around to look at her. "Police," she whispered. Sophia's eyes widened. She pressed a finger to her lips and motioned for Kasia to follow her. They crept out of the bedroom to a staircase hidden behind a door. It led them to an attic, a circular window at each end.

Sophia led her to one. She pointed to the house across a

small gap. "The roof," she said, unlatching the window and motioning towards the opening.

Kasia blanched. She could probably make it, but the fall was long. Another round of knocking, this time accompanied by Magda's protests. A man's voice rang out. "Sophia Worley. Detroit Police. Come out with your hands up." Kasia grabbed Sophia and pressed her lips against hers. Sophia gripped her arms when she pulled away.

Magda's scream rang out from downstairs. And then another voice: "Sophia Worley. You're harboring a fugitive, Andrew Kasowski. Both of you come out now with your hands up." They broke apart. Kasia watched Sophia compose herself as she crept down the stairs. She pulled her shoulders back, head high and indignant. Kasia could almost see her head toss as she called out, "What is the meaning of this?" The closed attic door muffled her anger.

Kasia perched on the windowsill, eyeing the distance to the next roof over. She'd have to jump to make it. Kasia gritted her teeth, willing her eyes away from the ground. If she looked down, she'd talk herself out of it.

She rocked back on her heels. In one swift movement, she swung herself forward and up, legs tensing and springing to drive her. The roof slammed into her stomach. Kasia had to press her lips together to hide the groan it drove from her. Her still-bruised ribs screamed, sending tears to her eyes. It took every ounce of strength she had to pull herself forward on her arms. Eventually, she got her feet gathered under her. She crept across the roof, as low as possible to avoid drawing attention. If she made it to the other side, she could shimmy down a drainpipe, take off through the yard.

She could still hear yelling behind her. Once she made it to the opposite edge, she paused, waiting for closer voices.

When she heard nothing, she ventured a glance around. No one.

The look almost made her want to stay put. The ground reeled up at her. Kasia thought she might vomit. Shoving it down, she found a drainpipe on a corner wall. She had no idea she could hold something so tightly, but somehow her feet safely touched the ground.

Kasia took off. Running was difficult, more of a half-limp, her hand clutched to her abused ribcage. But no sirens and no footsteps sounded behind her.

# Chapter Thirty-Five

By sheer force of habit, Kasia found her way back to Hamtramck. It was really the last place she should be. But the aimlessness she'd fought the day before worked like a compass now, pulling her back home.

She tried to be smart, stick to side streets. She dodged alley to alley. It was still early enough to be quiet in the neighborhood, but it would soon be bustling. Kasia had to find somewhere to hide.

Nothing could have prepared her for rounding a corner and nearly crashing into Christopher. The two stopped and gawked at each other for a moment, startled into stillness. "Jesus, Andy, what are you doing here?" her cousin said, wide-eyed. "You look like shit." Kasia glanced down. She was rumpled, her shirt untucked. She hadn't had time to bind, but her jacket helped to hide her breasts. "The police have been all over the place looking for you." He spoke in rapid bursts, almost excited.

"Yeah, I figured as much," Kasia said. "They hit the warehouse?"

"They tore it apart, Andrew. I don't know how Czeslaw's family is going to afford fixing it. They hit your mother's, and *my* mother's, and God knows how many of the guys."

Kasia's stomach sank. "Chris. I'm sorry. I didn't mean for any of this to happen."

"What the hell *did* happen? Your mother keeps saying you're not her son." Christopher shook his head. "Where'd she think you were getting the money?"

Christopher had been a kid when Kasia disappeared and "Andrew" returned from the war. She was the Andrew he knew, not her brother. And he'd idolized her and her gang, relied on her to get him out of scrapes. For a moment, she considered telling him everything. But there was no time, and it wasn't as important as what Kasia had to ask him.

"Chris." She gripped his shoulders. "I need you to look after my mother for me."

Her cousin's face darkened. "What do you mean? Where are you going?"

"I don't know." Kasia leaned in. "Listen to me. I need you to keep your nose clean. I'm not able to keep you out of trouble anymore. And I need you," she repeated, "to look after my mother."

"Are you going to jail?" Christopher suddenly looked like a child to Kasia. The excitement had faded from him. He slumped beneath her hold on his shoulders.

"Maybe," Kasia said. "Can you do what I said?"

"Yeah." Christopher's voice cracked. "Yeah, I can do that."

"Do you promise?" Kasia shook him as she spoke.

"I promise."

Kasia wrapped her arms around Christopher and squeezed him hard. He stiffened. They weren't a family that touched often. But all she could think about was Christopher when he was small, running around the neighborhood in short pants and ruffled hair. She'd always been able to make him laugh as a kid. She'd tell him the worst jokes she knew and swing him around until he screamed and his mother came to scold them. *I liked you better* before *the war*, she'd told Kasia pointedly. But she'd caught her aunt smiling when she thought Kasia and Christopher weren't looking. She might have disapproved of her rough-housing, but she kept Kasia's secret.

Kasia finally let her cousin go. "Thanks."

Chris lingered, awkward. "Good luck."

As she watched him leave, Kasia felt bile rise in her throat. Panic squeezed her lungs, hammered her heart. She leaned against a wall, feeling the cold brick bite into her skin. Kasia tried to push the fear down. She inhaled hard through her nose. She didn't calm, but she settled. At least enough to make a decision. Kasia wound her way through the familiar streets until she landed at her mother's front door.

Her key still worked. That was something, at least. Kasia braced herself to face the wreckage on the other side of the door.

It wasn't what Kasia anticipated. A broken leg hung off a table. Everything looked otherwise untouched. It could have been more than Kasia hoped for, but that table leg told a different story. One where her mother, unable to bear things being out of place, couldn't rest until there was little trace of the chaos. It broke Kasia's heart more than if she'd walked into a mess.

Her room, however, looked exactly as she'd suspected. Drawers were overturned and thrown aside. The bed and floor were buried beneath clothes, papers, photographs, and trinkets. Kasia hadn't left anything incriminating in her mother's house. It wasn't like she was accustomed to writing her plans down. Still, there was one thing that made her heart stop.

Kasia waded through the mess to her closet. She threw armfuls of clothes aside until she could kneel by the back wall. With a little effort, she loosened the baseboard and pulled it free. A gap beneath the wall, hardly wider than Kasia's hand, skimmed the space behind it. Kasia reached in, holding her breath. Her hand made contact with the cash. Kasia's eyes closed. She heaved a sigh and pulled it out. Then the next stack, and three more. The cops hadn't found it.

Her next task involved sifting through everything the cops had left scattered around the room. She picked up two dresses, appropriate underthings. Kasia changed into one of them and peered into her now-shattered mirror. Her reflection startled her. She couldn't remember the last time she'd worn a dress. It felt wrong. It made her skin itch. It was also incredibly out of date. It had been unfashionable when she'd last worn it; it was downright old-fashioned now. She looked like a religious fanatic.

Good. Maybe she'd lean into it. She tied a scarf around her head to hide her close-cropped hair. The other outfit, she packed, along with a small wad of bills pulled from one of the closet piles. Kasia found two envelopes in the kitchen. One, she stuffed with two of the bundles of cash and left on the counter. She thought about writing her mother a note. But writing was never one of Kasia's strengths, and she didn't know what to say. She put the remaining cash in the second envelope, and scrawled brief instructions on the outside: help Stan and Henry's families, and use the rest to repair the warehouse. She'd drop it on Crezlaw's porch on her way out of the neighborhood.

Kasia couldn't help but linger on the way out. She wanted to remember the peeling paint and the faded wallpaper. She wanted to remember the tree across the street. Most of all, she wanted to remember the familiarity, the shape of home.

# Chapter Thirty-Six

The boarding house Kasia chose was only blocks away from Sophia. It was a risk she shouldn't be taking. But the thought of being unable to reach her at a moment's notice was unbearable. Especially since she had no idea what happened after she fled Sophia's house.

Kasia spent the afternoon and evening pacing from wall to wall in her boarding house room. Every one of her edges was frayed. She hadn't prayed since childhood. She hardly remembered how. But she sent up prayer after prayer now that Sophia was safe. Kasia made promises in return she wasn't sure she could keep, or how interested a reasonable God would be with her reform. But she offered it up anyway, promised to be good.

She'd lost everything but Sophia. She couldn't bear the thought of the most devastating blow.

Kasia watched the clock tick down to midnight. As soon as it struck, she left for Sophia's house. She snuck to the back door and knocked. Magda answered several minutes later in her night clothes, bloodshot eyes betraying that she hadn't actually slept. For a moment, she seemed not to recognize Kasia in a dress. Once she did, her eyes widened. The maid pulled Kasia inside, tutting. "You shouldn't be here. The police are still looking for you. They might be watching the house."

"Where's Sophia?" Kasia should have appreciated Magda's concern for her, but there was only one topic on her mind.

Magda eyed her carefully. "Sophia was arrested earlier. The police were looking for you, but when she didn't cooperate... well, things became heated."

Kasia blanched. "She's in jail?"

The maid clasped her shoulders tightly, as if to hold her to the ground. "Her lawyer is there, working on bail. There's nothing for you to do."

Kasia broke away from Magda's grip. She clutched the wall, light-headed. Magda placed a comforting hand on her back, and Kasia fought not to shrug away the touch. "I need to see her. Where is she being held?"

Magda's hand tensed. "No. It's too dangerous for both of you."

The warning tone caught Kasia's attention. Magda was right. "Then after she's out. I can come back tomorrow."

"*No.*" Magda sounded exasperated now. "You can't come back here, and she can't go to you. You need to meet somewhere. Can you get to Belle Isle in two days?" Kasia nodded. "Good. Meet her at noon near the bandstand. I'll let her know."

"Thank you," Kasia said. It was hard to lift her eyes off the floor.

Kasia went back to the boarding house, but hardly slept.

Over and over, she saw the fear in Sophia's eyes when the cops called her name. She saw Henry and Stan in flashes, too, as if they loomed by her bed, their eyes boring into her filthy soul. Overwhelming shame knotted her stomach every time she pictured their faces. She spent the next day in her room, coming out only to scrounge up leftovers from the kitchen after dinner. Kasia slept little that night as well. She gave up at sunrise. Instead, she bathed and changed into her only other dress—equally dowdy, but clean. It would take her two hours to walk to Belle Isle. She had plenty of time. She set off anyway. Moving was easier than sitting still.

The morning was chilly, but not unbearable. Some of the trees Kasia passed held dainty green buds. It would have been a pleasant walk in any other circumstance. But circumstances being what they were, Kasia was too tormented to notice. She had no idea what to do or where to go. After losing her gang, Kasia knew she should have pivoted without a second thought. New place, next plan. Sophia limited her options. Not just her arrest, although the thought filled Kasia with fury. She couldn't leave Sophia behind without telling her what she planned.

Kasia found the bandstand well before noon. It was empty, but passed occasionally by the crowd meandering around the park. To blend in, Kasia joined them. She found places to sit as she wandered. She kept her head down, slouched, and hoped to be forgettable.

When it was finally time to meet Sophia, Kasia's heart quickened. At the stroke of noon, she found her. Sophia wore a brown hat and coat and a simple, calf-length cream dress. It was plainer than her usual style, and she faced away from Kasia, but she recognized her immediately. Kasia stood beside her. Stretching her fingers, she brushed against

Sophia's hand. Sophia caught her and gave her hand a squeeze before clasping her own in front of her. "I'm so glad to see you," Sophia whispered, still staring ahead.

Kasia felt tears pressing inside her eyes. "Are you alright?"

Sophia chuckled. "Oh, yes. James's ex-boyfriend is an excellent lawyer. I've used him for years."

Kasia dared a glance at Sophia's face. Behind several layers of powder, mottled blue and purple skin peered through. Kasia turned Sophia to face her, taking her cheeks in her hands. Her right eye was swollen half-shut. Lipstick covered a split lip, and bruises scattered her cheeks and jaw. "Jesus Christ. They hit you?" Her rage boiled to the surface.

Sophia's eyes fell. "Harding had a score to settle. In fairness, I wasn't going quietly."

"He can't do that to you." Kasia gripped Sophia's arm and pulled the sleeve of her coat up. Her skin was covered in bruises, some in the shape of purple fingerprints.

Sophia pulled away. "Don't, Kasia." She shook her head. "You don't need to chase any more trouble."

Kasia glared down at Sophia. "His cops killed Henry and Stan. And now this? I'm not letting him get away with it."

The woman remained impassive. She had the look she got when her heels dug in. "Please, Kasia. Let it go. Let Harding go. I don't want you in more danger than you're already in. Please. For me."

Kasia bit back her fury and tucked a stray curl behind Sophia's ear. Pushing her harder would result in a standoff. They didn't have time for that. Kasia released a long breath. "Alright." Sophia's eyes widened; she hadn't expected Kasia to relent. "You're right. We're in enough trouble." Kasia ran a gentle hand over Sophia's shoulder. "Besides, we need to spend the time we have figuring out what's next." When Sophia didn't answer, Kasia continued. "I'm wanted by the cops. I can't stay here."

Sophia looked up at Kasia, eyes huge and watery. She snuck her fingers between Kasia's and squeezed them gently. "But where will you go?"

"I have no idea," Kasia said. "Maybe out West. I could try California."

"You have connections in California?" Sophia asked.

"I don't have a single connection outside this city," Kasia said. "For me, anywhere is starting from nothing." She glanced behind them to make sure no one was watching before gently stroking Sophia's bruised cheek with her thumb. "Unless you come with me."

Sophia's brows rose, but Kasia pressed on. It was a long shot, but she knew, deep in her marrow, that if she didn't try she'd regret it forever. "I know I don't have a single thing to offer you. No money, no connections, no family name. But I'll do everything I can to provide for us and keep you safe. I promise. I don't know what a life with you would look like. I can't picture anything that beautiful. But I know I want to try."

Sophia bit her lip, and Kasia's heart sank. She hadn't thought Sophia would go with her, not really. She was probably just another one of Sophia's flings. But it stuck in her chest like a knife. Sophia was silent for an eternal, agonizing minute, her eyes wandering over Kasia's face. When she took in a breath, Kasia braced herself for rejection.

"I have an idea," Sophia said. "But I need to make arrangements."

"Arrangements?"

"Could you be ready in two weeks?"

"For what?" Kasia said.

"To leave."

Kasia's brows furrowed. "Of course. But... do you mean...."

"I'm coming with you," Sophia said.

Kasia's eyes widened. Despite the fact that she'd asked, part of her couldn't believe Sophia meant it. She had so much more to leave behind than Kasia. "You're sure?"

Sophia pinned her eyes on the bandstand in front of them. "I've lost the Lavender. Harding's made it clear that I can't so much as sneeze without consequence. I've lost my freedom here, even if they decide not to put me in prison. Getting out is the only way to preserve it." She turned to look at Kasia. "And I want that freedom with you."

Kasia flushed, her brain a tangle of thought that she couldn't translate into words.

"I'm not sure I can pull off what I have in mind." Sophia's look was distant now, planning. "It's not safe to contact me, Kasia," Sophia continued. She was right, but Kasia's heart sank. "I'll get you a note with the date we leave. Until then, you need to stay safe."

Kasia frowned. "But where are we going?"

"I don't want to say too much. Not while I'm still figuring it out myself. You have to trust me." Sophia tilted her head. "You're really sure that you can leave everything behind? I've done it before. It's not easy."

"If you're with me, there's nothing back home to miss," Kasia said.

She watched as a lovely flush crept up Sophia's cheeks. "You say that now," Sophia said. "You may be surprised what you end up missing."

"I look forward to finding out," Kasia answered. She caught Sophia's pinky in hers for a brief, sweet moment.

Sophia looked up at her with pleading eyes. "Promise

me you'll stay out of trouble, Kasia," she said. "Promise you won't do anything stupid. Nothing that could keep you from me."

Kasia smiled reassuringly. "Just tell me when and where. Until then, I'll keep my nose clean. No matter what, I'll meet you."

# Chapter Thirty-Seven

She'd lied to Sophia. She hadn't dropped her grudge against Harding. She'd seen men sucker punch a cop square in the nose and come out the other end in better shape. Kasia could understand holding a grudge—Harding *had* walked in on Sophia with his wife—but this? Taking advantage of the fray to beat a woman to the ground?

And Harding hadn't just hurt Sophia—his men were the reason Henry and Stan were dead. Their family and friends, and Kasia herself, were in the vise grip of loss that would last a lifetime. That was the thing about grief. You never really forgot it, never moved past it completely. There were better and worse days, but Andrew always haunted her thoughts. Now Stan and Henry would, too.

Kasia had nothing but time on her hands. That was dangerous in the best circumstances. Now it gave her time to brood. She paced the tiny room of her boarding house, four staccato steps from wall to wall. Her steps synchronized with her heartbeat—rapid strides each time her guilt, shame, and grief flared again and again. First Sophia's face floated in front of her—then Henry, then Stan, then Andrew. *I'm sorry,* she whispered each time. *I'm so sorry.*

She preferred the moments of rage. It gripped her with burning tension, roiled in her stomach, flared into her chest, drew her shoulders tight. All her other feelings made her want to run. Rage, she could chew on. It promised her action.

She just didn't know what yet.

Three startling bangs on her floor broke the spell. "Shut the fuck up," another boarder's muffled voice shouted from below. Their patience for her pacing had clearly worn thin. Kasia dropped to her knees. She thought about yelling back, but couldn't find the energy. Instead, she curled up on her side, half on the grimy little rug by her bed and half on the worn hardwood. She didn't realize until the cold wood met her skin that tears soaked her face down to the collar of her dress.

*Useless,* she thought. *Tears are useless.* They wouldn't bring Henry or Stan back. They wouldn't heal Sophia's bruises or keep her safe from Harding. She pulled herself back to sitting and wiped her running nose with the sleeve of her dress. Harding's men pulled the trigger, and Harding himself beat Sophia the moment he had an excuse. But Kasia was at the center of it all. She was responsible for their deaths. She was responsible for Sophia's pain. That meant it was her responsibility to avenge it.

It comforted her. All her sorrow had a face and a name: Chief Harding. She turned the thought over, savoring the idea of retaliation. It tasted bittersweet, but it was better than uselessness. She'd promised Sophia to stay out of trouble—but how could she, with such a responsibility on her shoulders? Maybe she didn't have to know. Maybe if she did, she'd understand.

Vengeance had its teeth in her now. It was a familiar bite, one she knew well during her decade running Hamtramck. She relished the way its venom seeped into her veins. It gave her direction, purpose. The determination she thought she'd lost along with her gang was, in fact, alive and well.

Kasia pulled herself off the floor and sat at the beaten desk by her room's one window. She folded her arms across the desktop, eyes unfocused, immense calculations behind them. A hundred plans unfolded at once. Some were quick and efficient. Others were pure fantasy, an indulgence of ideal revenge. She savored those, even knowing they were impossible. But no matter how many times she turned them over in her mind, she ran into the same problem: gaps in information. Some of her questions could be answered by following Harding around for a week, but that was asking to be caught. She might have lied to Sophia about keeping out of trouble, but she had to at least try to keep her promise to meet her.

She needed information. One man had it. She had to talk to Sam.

It would be hard to track him down. He was lying low. It was the smart thing to do. But she'd worked with him for years. She knew where he liked to hang out, or at least where his friends did. She didn't have her clothes—Andrew's clothes—with her, which made things harder. But she asked around as Andrew's sister. Some people seemed suspicious; they should be, she thought. But a couple of people pointed her in Sam's direction. She found him in the back of a butcher shop owned by one of his friends.

Confusion passed over his face when she walked in. After a moment, Sam guffawed. Tears streamed down his face as he looked at her. Kasia stood, impassive, watching

Sam's shoulders rise and fall. "Jesus Christ, Andy," he said. "I'd heard some crazy rumors, but nothing like this. You're a woman now?"

"Something like that." Kasia stared Sam down, waiting for his amusement to pass. Sam wiped at his eyes. "I need all the information you have on the Chief."

"What happened to your source? And for that matter, what happened to your boys? Czeslaw said you disappeared."

"I don't have time for that," Kasia said. "I want Harding dead, and I'll do it myself."

Sam's face fell, his mouth gaping open. "Jesus, Andy. That's a suicide mission."

"Just tell me everything you know about him. Where he lives, his routines. Basics. I know you've done the legwork on all of it. You just don't want the heat of being the one to off him, or you wouldn't need blackmail to keep him in check. So tell me what I need to know and let me do the rest."

Sam picked up a pen and rolled it around in his fist. "I don't want your shit connected to me. You already got busted once."

"Which means I'm not working for you anymore," Kasia said. "And I've got motive to take him out on my own. He destroyed my business." She took a step towards Sam. "Harding will be out of your hair. You might get someone in his place more willing to play ball."

Sam clicked his tongue. "Alright. You want to do this, it's on your head. If you get caught, you better play up the unhinged killer working alone angle. Keep me out of it. This," he said, gesturing to Kasia, "whatever is happening here, is a good start."

Kasia ignored the last comment, her expression unchanging. "Tell me everything you know about him."

Sam relented. He knew the Chief's routine down to the minute. It wasn't hard; he didn't go out much, just work and home or his summer house, with an occasional visit to a restaurant with his wife or to political events. Harding had cops posted around his house at all times. He always traveled with two. Kasia remembered that from his visit to the paper supply. Figuring out his next outing would take time she didn't have, and it would be doubly risky trying to take him down in public. It would have to be his house, somehow avoiding the cops stationed there for security, or en route to work, with a driver and two bodyguards. Neither was optimal.

But it gave Kasia options. Something to chew on while she waited for Sophia's message. Something to chase out her memories, which always brought the nausea and heat of shame. Distraction. Direction. A goal. A plan. The kind of thing Kasia thrived on.

Usually.

An uneasiness she couldn't shake crept in. It whispered to her about broken promises. She kept thinking of Sophia's words: *What I see is a death wish.* Maybe she was right. Maybe Kasia spent her life obsessively pushing the border that separated her and hell. Maybe it had finally caught up to her, breathing its rotten breath down her neck. *What is it you really want, Kasia?* Sophia's voice echoed. The same answers she'd always had rose first. To keep her promise to her brother. To pay off her mother's house. Her own gang. Respect. The security of money. Becoming a Purple. But what good was any of it now? She'd kept her promise as best she could. She'd paid off the house, and left her mother with enough to get by, with her cousin's help just in case. Everything else was gone. No more gang, no more respect. Most of her money went to her mother and her friend's grieving families, and she'd never be a Purple.

Then what did she want? *Sophia*, Kasia thought. *I want Sophia*. If God himself came down from heaven and handed her back everything she'd lost, she'd trade it in a heartbeat if it meant Sophia was safe, sound, and hers. And the last part was negotiable. She'd settle for a glimpse of her now and then. Hell, if she had to she'd trade never seeing her again, ever, for a guarantee that Sophia was safe.

Vengeance bit down harder. Kasia welcomed the blaze of her fury. The heat tearing through her was steadying. If Sophia was safer with Harding gone, she had no choice. And if death came for Kasia instead, she hoped Sophia would leave without her.

# Chapter Thirty-Eight

Twelve days passed without word from Sophia. When Kasia wasn't puzzling out how to get to Harding, she worried that silence was the only message Sophia would send. Heart twisting, Kasia pictured Sophia running off alone to put distance between them. Kasia could hardly blame her if she did. She'd brought her nothing but chaos. It was almost a relief, she told herself. Sophia was safer without her.

But Sophia's letter finally arrived in a cream envelope marked with the fake name she'd checked into the boarding house under, dropped off with the matron who ran it. She hadn't disappeared. Relief flooded Kasia as she turned the letter over in her hands. The firm, folded paper held only a date and time—two days from now, in the early hours of the morning—and a place. Cross-streets just outside the city. Kasia held the letter to her nose, imagining she could catch a drift of Sophia's perfume on the page. Two long days until she could see Sophia again.

That gave her a deadline. It felt like the hours before she'd see Sophia would stretch on forever, but she had to work fast. She had one day to complete her plan, and another to execute.

She paced her room again, ignoring her downstairs neighbor's protests. He wouldn't have to put up with her for long anyway, however her plan went. She'd either be with Sophia or in a morgue. She had a feeling she knew which one her neighbor would prefer.

Kasia had thought of a hundred plans by now. The trick was picking one, fleshing it out, making it real. The nagging voice in her head—Sophia's voice, really—made it harder. But she forced herself to focus. There wasn't time for anything but ambition, venom, and forethought. It was a familiar groove into which her body could nestle. It felt good. Really good. She turned each plan over in her head, waiting until she landed on the one that made her drop into her body. Her hands and feet hummed with it. She sat up straighter, bolstered by the *rightness* of it burning in her core.

She waited until the night before she was supposed to meet Sophia to find Harding's neighborhood. Better for making a quick getaway, if the plan went right. If it all went sideways, the timing was even better. Sophia was already prepared to leave.

The night was chilly and overcast, the only light pooling beneath streetlamps that she skirted. The familiar press of her gun inside her coat was comforting, even as her heart hammered. She'd cut the hem of her dress up to mid-calf, hoping it would keep the fabric out of her way. Kasia hated that she didn't have pants to work in.

*You shouldn't be working at all,* Sophia's voice admonished. Kasia shook the voice from her head. She thought of Stan and Henry and their families beside their graves. She thought of Sophia's face covered in bruises, her swollen eye and cut lip, and worse—the fear in her expression when Kasia held her chin. Her stomach clenched, hot and purifying. She couldn't turn back. Whether Sophia wanted it or not, she deserved revenge. So did Henry and Stan.

When she got close to Harding's house, she started cutting through backyards. She didn't mind taking the long way around fences or detouring for thick gardens and bushes. Kasia wanted a little extra distance. Better to have more room and a slow approach.

Once she got close enough to see the roof poking up from behind a tree, she crouched. Kasia's eyes roamed between the house and her surroundings as she crept from cover to cover. The night clung to her in eerie silence. The back of Harding's house loomed above her, as quiet and still as its surroundings. There wasn't much to hide her here. She curled behind the neighbor's bushes, looking into open lawn.

A flicker of motion caught her attention. A cop sitting in a chair on Harding's back patio, deep in the shadows. Kasia's heart leapt to her mouth. She might not have noticed him if he hadn't rubbed his eyes, even looking for him. Kasia would've been caught before she'd even started, all her plans shot to nothing. *It's all for nothing if you're dead,* Sophia's voice said.

*This is* for *you, for fuck's sake,* Kasia shot back in her head. Her blood roiled, pressure building in her chest. She was starting to feel insane, arguing with herself in Sophia's voice. She brushed it off and squinted harder into the dark. Harding stationed one man in the front, and one in the back. Kasia couldn't afford to alert both with a gunshot. She pulled her knife from her boot.

Kasia glanced at the ground around her. The yard was perfectly manicured. Not a stone to throw in sight. *Shit.*

The hedge she hid behind was long, though, a straight line of neatly trimmed branches just sprouting spring leaves. If she moved fast enough, it might provide both cover and a lure. It was risky, but she had few other options at her disposal.

*You could leave,* Sophia's voice said.

Kasia shook her head, as if Sophia was around to see it. *I'm not backing out now.*

Kasia found a spot at the edge of the hedge furthest from the door and shook it gently, the branches rustling. At first, she heard nothing, no movement from the cop on duty. *Did he fall asleep?* Kasia shifted her weight between her feet, irritated. After a minute, she shook the branches again. This time, she heard the soft crunch of footsteps on dead grass. Kasia slipped towards the other end of the hedge, as quietly as she could, until she could round the corner and hide in the darkness at the edge of the bushes. She held her breath as the guard passed her hiding spot, his gun at the ready.

The cop pulled a flashlight from his jacket and flooded the space behind the bushes she'd shaken with light. Kasia pulled her limbs around her, making herself as small as possible behind the short edge of the hedge behind him. He passed the light over the neighbor's yard, squinting into the emptiness. Finally, he turned towards Harding's other neighbors, by the opposite end of the hedge. Now that his back was to her, she crept behind him, as close as she dared. And in one motion, she sprang and wrapped her arms around him, the knife pinned across his throat.

Kasia pulled with all her weight as she parted his skin with the knife. The layers of muscle in his neck resisted the edge, despite its wicked sharpness. He clawed her wrist before she could complete the cut, wrenched the knife to angle it up. But she'd gotten deep enough. *My God, the blood*, Kasia thought. It coated her hand, soaked her jacket up to the elbow. It pumped out of the man in waves, coated his front, pooled on his feet. He fell to his knees. Kasia watched him crumple to the ground.

It was too dark to see his blood soak into the dead grass. But Kasia could swear she saw it, anyway. Frozen, she watched his twitching limbs still, his breath gurgling from him in wet gasps before it stopped entirely.

Kasia recoiled, the knife falling from her hand. She had long left squeamishness behind. Her work required it. But this was different. She'd killed a man and watched him die. Not Harding, not a rival, not someone who threatened to expose her secret, but a stranger whose death came only because he didn't pay enough attention on guard duty. She realized too late that it turned her stomach.

She squatted down, head between her knees to pull in gulping breaths. She retrieved her knife and held it between shaking fingers. *Is this who I am now?* The sight of the dead man made her stomach clench, bile rushing to her mouth. She spat beside the body, trying to regain control of her own. But Sophia's battered face rose in her mind again, flared white-hot in her veins. *I'm already a killer.* Leaving wouldn't bring the guard back, and it wasn't a satisfying exchange for the lives of her friends.

She pulled herself shakily to her feet and turned to Harding's back door. From her pocket, she pulled a couple tools she'd saved from her gang's early days. Kasia was out of practice, but she let the feeling of the lock picks in her hands guide her. It took a minute—and minutes were precious—but eventually the pins fell into place, and the lock turned. Kasia opened the door inch by inch and closed it behind her just as carefully.

She was standing in Harding's kitchen.

The quiet of the room crushed her from all sides. She froze. The image of the cop outside, blood oozing between his fingers as he desperately held his open neck, felt like a film projected into the surrounding dark. Harding had a wife who was sleeping soundly. Kasia had no intention of touching her. But she'd find him dead. She might even hear him die, or watch it. She'd have it seared into her memory the way the guard's death was surely seared in hers.

It wasn't that she couldn't get over the idea that the Chief's family would mourn. Henry and Stan's families mourned plenty. But thinking of Harding's wife reminded her of Sophia. She'd promised to stay out of trouble. But here she was, more blood on her hands than ever.

Kasia's fear of losing her seared her heart. Did it sear Sophia's, too? She'd pleaded for Kasia to let Harding go.

*What do you want, Kasia?* She looked to the back door, then into the dark house. She thought of Sophia's bruised face, the lingering proof of Harding's willingness to hurt her and Kasia's failure to protect her. She thought of her mother's grief and disappointment. She thought of her former friends, mourning Stan and Henry. She thought of her brother and the crimes that would be forever attached to his name. Thief. Bootlegger. Sodomite. Gang leader. Cop-killer.

The gun in her jacket laid heavy against her chest. She'd thought that after her first kill, the next would be easier. Especially Harding, after what he'd said to her and done to Sophia. Instead, she'd never been so uncertain. She couldn't move forward or take back anything that had already been done.

*What do you want, Kasia?*
*Not this.*

It hit her like a blow to the chest, knocking her to her hands and knees. She stifled a sob with a hand pushed so hard over her mouth that her nails dug crescents into her cheeks. This was who she was. A murderer and a liar, and somehow a coward as well.

*What do you want, Kasia?*

*Sophia. Just Sophia.*

There it was, so clear in front of her now. The chasm between who she was and what she wanted. What Sophia deserved. An insurmountable distance between them.

She knew what she should do. What her old self would do, before she became this lovesick mess of a woman. Pull herself off the floor, find Harding, take him out. Disappear into the night. Not to join Sophia, but to keep herself as far away as possible.

Before. There was before Sophia, and there was after. Something in her had changed—for the better or the worse, Kasia didn't know. Something fundamental. Something she'd thought untouchable.

*I want Sophia.*

She wanted her more than she wanted anything. She knew that much. More than she'd ever wanted money, power, or a place in the Purple Gang. She wanted to keep Sophia safe and happy. She wanted Sophia to trust her, to know that she'd keep her promises.

*I want Sophia.*

The poison in her blood spoke up. *More than justice?*

Kasia thought of Stan and Henry. She thought of the police destroying her mother's home. She thought of Sophia's battered face. Rage contorted her, back arching high. Her hands gripped at the slick kitchen tile.

*Yes.* It was Andrew's voice she heard now. Somewhere along the way, she'd forgotten the weight of a promise made in love. But for all her faults—for all the things she'd done, for all the things she'd become—that was her, too. She'd kept a promise he hadn't asked her to make.

She *was* a coward. Not because she was on her hands and knees on Harding's kitchen floor. Not because she couldn't get the dead man in the yard out of her mind. But because it wasn't vengeance for anyone else she was seeking. Henry and Stan couldn't ask for it. Sophia didn't want it in the first place.

No. She was a coward because what she wanted from vengeance wasn't vengeance at all. She'd wanted to prove who she was: someone to fear. Someone untouchable. Someone she'd been once. Someone she wasn't anymore.

She didn't know who she was now. *That* was losing everything.

Almost everything.

In a few hours, Sophia would be waiting for her at an intersection outside of town. Kasia didn't know where they were going or what she would do there. She had no idea what her life would look like, or who she'd become inside it.

And suddenly, this thing—so terrifying, so overwhelming it drove her through Harding's door—didn't matter.

Whoever Kasia had been, it wouldn't end by killing Harding. Whoever Kasia could be, it would start with keeping her promise to Sophia.

# Chapter Thirty-Nine

Kasia flung open the back door and ran. She left it gaping behind her. She ran until the blood rushing through her head drowned out the sound of her gasping breaths. She ran until her thighs and stomach cramped and her calves curled into knots. She ran until her body refused one more stride, forcing her to slow to a shuffling walk, clenching her side. Kasia gulped in air, turned her face towards the starless sky.

She walked farther than she thought possible before she found a cab to hail. She took off her jacket before she got in, wrapping the parts coated in dried blood tightly inside the rest and covering her bloodied hand. The cab would cost the rest of the money she had. She was truly starting over with nothing.

She found Sophia at the cross-streets as planned. Sophia waited next to a running car, suitcases tied to the roof and piled next to her feet. She was bundled in fur, her hair perfectly in place, with red lipstick that stood out even in the dim light of pre-dawn. Kasia embraced her wordlessly. The walk brought plenty of time for regrets to sink in. Part of her still wished she'd killed Harding when she had the chance. But the warmth of Sophia against her reminded her why she'd done what she had.

"It's cold, why aren't you wearing your coat?" Sophia asked as she pulled away. Kasia's eyes locked to the ground as Sophia pulled it from her arm. The blood on her hand caught Sophia's attention. She turned it over, looking for a wound. Sophia paled, her eyes wide as they lifted to Kasia's face. "What happened?"

Kasia shook her head. "You don't need to know." She brushed Sophia's cheek. "Let me protect you."

"Protect me?" Sophia dropped her hand. "Is this the way you protect me? After I asked you to keep yourself safe?"

"You're right," Kasia acceded immediately. "You're right." She swallowed hard. How the hell could she possibly explain? "I didn't kill Harding." Sophia raised an eyebrow, looking pointedly down at the blood on Kasia's hands. "I... didn't keep my promise, either. Not at first." Sophia looked from Kasia to the running car, brows knitted deep. Kasia knew she was second-guessing her choices. *She should be*, Kasia thought. But Kasia had to try. She couldn't do anything else.

"You're the most important thing in the world to me, Sophia. I should never have compromised that." Sophia's questioning gaze roamed over Kasia's face. Words tumbled out of Kasia's mouth, voice shaking. "I went to Harding's house. I was standing inside his kitchen, even. I convinced myself it was the right thing. For you, and for Henry and Stan. It wasn't. I was scared, and angry, and I didn't know what else to do. I didn't know who else to be. I broke your trust, and if you hate me for it, it's well-deserved. If you leave right now, I'd understand. In fact, it's probably the right thing to do."

Kasia took a deep breath. "But I left because he doesn't matter. Not like you. Nothing matters like you, and becoming someone you deserve to have by your side. Everything else, I can let go. I can't let go of you." She wrapped her arms around Sophia's waist. "I love you, Sophia. Please."

The words felt awkward in her mouth. She meant every syllable of it, with her whole heart. Every part of her belonged to this woman. The words were simply unfamiliar. Rarely said among her family, and she'd never had the occasion to say them to anyone else.

Sophia's face softened. It gave Kasia a flicker of hope. But the silence as Sophia gazed up at her felt interminable. She looked back at Kasia's hand, running her thumb over the brown blood that stained her cuticles.

Sophia looked up and gripped Kasia's chin. "You broke your promise once already. I need something more than a promise now."

Kasia wasn't sure what that meant. But she dropped to her knees in front of Sophia, clasping her hands in her own. "Before you, I couldn't mourn. Every lick I've taken, I've stood back up. An eye for an eye. It's the only justice I've had. And it's the only thing I've known how to do."

Kasia squeezed her hands. "I won't make more promises I can't keep. I'll always want to protect you. But I do know that things are different than they were before you. You've reshaped me. I don't want the things I've had. And I don't want to do the things I've always done."

"What do you want?" Sophia asked. Kasia almost laughed. If only Sophia knew how often she'd asked herself exactly that in Sophia's voice.

"Other than you? I have no idea. But I *do* want something else. I can't picture it, not fully, because I don't know what else is possible. To be somewhere with you where we're safe. To live as myself, somehow, at least sometimes. To know what I like, not just what I'm responsible for. To find something like a happy life. A long life, if I'm lucky. With you."

Sophia tugged Kasia back to her feet. She stretched to kiss one corner of Kasia's mouth, then the other. "You're truly ready to start over?" Sophia whispered against her mouth. "Together?"

"Together." Kasia pressed her lips to Sophia's. Sophia softened in her arms, lingering in the press of their mouths.

"I suppose I always knew you had blood on your hands," Sophia murmured. After a moment, she pressed her palm into Kasia's cheek. "I love you too, you fool. But I can't have you causing this kind of trouble in Paris."

Kasia blinked. "Paris?"

"Paris."

Sophia reluctantly pulled away from Kasia's arms to knock on a window of the car. "I've got friends there, women like us. They write and host salons. They'll help us get on our feet." She stroked Kasia's cheek. "They live... more openly there. More than we can here. I hope... I hope I can help you find the things you want. Not just with me. But in whatever shape your wants take, when you have words for them."

They broke apart as the driver trotted around the car to open the door. Sophia grabbed a small suitcase from the pile around her and gestured to the driver. "Not this one, but the rest can go in the trunk. Thank you." She turned back to Kasia. "You're lucky I brought you some clothes. What have you done to your dress?"

Kasia looked down at her ragged hem. "I, uh...took it up a little. It looks better this way." She flashed Sophia a grin.

Sophia rolled her eyes. "I brought suits for you. I hope that's alright."

"That's perfect." Kasia was eager to shed her dress for good.

They piled into the backseat. Sophia tucked herself in against Kasia's shoulder. "I missed you, Kasia."

A smile warmed Kasia's face. "Good. You'll be seeing an awful lot of me from now on."

The city grew distant behind them. Kasia thought of her neighborhood, her mother, her friends, her career, all growing smaller and smaller. Her heart ached already. She'd lost them before she set out to start over, but it was another thing to leave them behind.

Sophia's warm breath on her neck brought her back. Her new life was open, unknowable. But it had Sophia in it. That was enough.

# Epilogue

The steamer pulled away from the New York pier with a long, low whistle. Kasia stood next to Sophia, hand in hand on the deck. People lined up along the rails to wave to the crowd gathered in the harbor. Sophia and Kasia waved too, laughing, even with no one there to wave to.

Sophia had filled Kasia in during their travels. She'd signed over her home to Magda, along with almost everything in it. Magda thought she could get a few things over to her eventually. Her friends in Paris would keep them for a few weeks while they sorted out a home. Sophia wasn't fluent in French, but she did well enough. She had enough money to keep them afloat for a while as they settled in.

The thought of living in another country where she spoke none of the language made Kasia antsy. But Sophia's confidence soothed her. She turned to watch Sophia, wearing a white dress trimmed in blue, no jacket to impede her enjoyment of the sun on her bare shoulders, a broad grin on her face as she waved. Sophia turned to Kasia, looking breathless with joy and squinting into the light.

Kasia smiled. It was the most beautiful sight she could imagine.

Sophia leaned in and brushed her lips over Kasia's cheek. "If anyone asks," Sophia purred in her ear, "you're my husband."

Kasia cupped Sophia's chin. "Am I?"

"Oh, yes," Sophia said, her eyes still sparkling. "Newly-weds on our honeymoon."

Kasia kissed her, not caring that they were in the middle of a crowd. "I'm a lucky son of a bitch, then."

Paris loomed large, but as far as Kasia was concerned, the whole world could fit into her arms in the shape of Sophia Worley.

# Acknowledgments

To my wonderful parents (all four of you!) - thank you for your loving, steady support. I'm incredibly lucky to have you, and you helped make this book possible. Thanks for being so proud of my writing that you want to read my hyper-niche lesbian romance. I hope you skipped the sex scene.

C - Thank you for your support during this entire project. I appreciated your alpha reads, your advice, and your enthusiasm. You're my biggest supporter and loudest cheerleader. I can't thank you enough for that. I love you.

T - My writing partner and literary guru. You always know niche classics that will change my life and improve my writing. Thanks for the conversations we have that challenge me to grow as a writer, and for your wonderful feedback on my work.

For all my beta readers, this wouldn't have been the same book without you. Thank you so much for your time and your feedback. I'd like to thank two beta readers in particular whose advice was invaluable to the book:

Cozy Dubois: your notes were not only incredibly thorough, it felt like they pulled the issues I knew I existed but couldn't identify directly from the recesses of my brain.

Your manuscript notes redefined how I approached the book, and it's much stronger for it.

Chelsea: Your feedback gave me the courage to write the story the way that I wanted it told. You immediately picked up where I'd made changes to the plot based on feedback I wasn't sure worked, but was afraid my own interpretation of the story wasn't good enough. Thanks for encouraging me to write Kasia's character development the way I'd originally envisioned it.

Special thanks to all my friends who put up with me talking about the book for months. I'm so lucky to have your encouragement and support. One of the book's themes is the power of community, and I'm blessed to have you as mine.